FLYING TOO HIGH

While walking the wings of a Tiger Moth plane in full flight should be enough excitement for most people, for Phryne Fisher, amateur detective and woman of mystery, it's merely the appetizer for greater thrills. For this 1920s glamorous detective flies even higher, handling a murder, a kidnapping and the usual array of beautiful young men with consummate ease – and all before it's time to adjourn to the Queenscliff Hotel for breakfast!

FLYING TOO HIGH

FLYING
TOO HIGH

by

Kerry Greenwood

Magna Large Print Books
Long Preston, North Yorkshire,
BD23 4ND, England.

British Library Cataloguing in Publication Data.

Greenwood, Kerry
    Flying too high.

    A catalogue record of this book is
    available from the British Library

    ISBN   978-0-7505-3830-5

First published in the UK by C&R Crime,
an imprint of Constable & Robinson Ltd., 2013

Published in Large Print 2014 by arrangement with
Constable & Robinson Ltd.

Magna Large Print is an imprint of Library Magna Books Ltd.

Printed and bound in Great Britain by
T.J. (International) Ltd., Cornwall, PL28 8RW

To David Lewis John Greagg
My own dear darling

Flying too high with some girl in the sky
Is my idea of nothing to do
But I get a kick out of you

'I Get A Kick Out Of You', Cole Porter

CHAPTER ONE

A sad tale's best for Winter
The Winter's Tale, Shakespeare

Candida Alice Maldon was being a bad girl. Firstly, she had not told anyone that she had found a threepence on the street. Secondly, she had not mentioned to anyone in the house that she was going out, because she knew that she would not be allowed. Thirdly, since she had lost one of her teeth, she was not supposed to be eating sweets, anyway.

The consciousness of wrongdoing had never stopped Candida from doing anything she wanted. She was prepared to be punished, and even prepared to feel sorry. Later. She approached the sweet-shop counter, clutching her threepence in her hand, and stared at the treasures within. Laid out, like those Egyptian treasures her father had shown her photos of in the paper, were sweets enough to give the whole world toothache.

There were red and green toffee umbrellas

and toffee horses on a stick. There were jelly-beans and jelly-babies and snakes in lots of colours, and lolly bananas and snow-balls and acid drops. These had the advantage that they were twenty-four a penny, but they were too sour for Candida's taste. She dismissed wine-gums as too gluey and musk sticks as too crumbly, and humbugs as too peppery. She considered boiled lollies in all the colours of the millefiore brooch which her grandmother wore, and barley-sugar in long, glassy canes. There were ring sticks with real rings around them, and rainbow balls and honeybears and chocolate toffs. Candida breathed heavily on the glass and wiped it with her sleeve.

'What would you like, dear?' asked the shopkeeper.

'My name is Candida,' the child informed her, 'and I have threepence. I would like a ha'porth of honeybears, a ha'porth of coffee buds, a ha'porth of mint-leaves, a ha'porth of silver sticks ... a ha'porth of umbrellas and a ha'porth of bananas.'

'There you are, Miss Candida,' said the shopkeeper, accepting the sweaty, warm coin. 'Here are your lollies. Don't eat them all at once!'

Candida walked out of the shop, and

began to trail her way home. She was not in a hurry because no one knew she was gone.

She was hopping in and out of the gutter, as she had been expressly forbidden to do, when a car drew up beside her. It was a black car shaped like a beetle. Nothing like her father's little Austin. Candida looked up with a start.

'Candida! There you are! Your daddy sent me to look for you. Where have you been?' A woman opened the car door and extended a hand.

Candida stepped closer to look. The woman had yellow hair and Candida did not like her smile.

'Come along now, dear. We'll take you home.'

'I don't believe you,' Candida said clearly. 'I don't believe my daddy sent you. I shall tell him you're a liar,' and she jumped back onto the pavement to run home. But someone in the back of the car was too quick. She was seized by strong hands and an odd-smelling handkerchief was clamped over her face. Then the world went dark green.

Phryne Fisher was enduring afternoon tea at the Traveller's Club with Mrs William McNaughton for a special reason. This did

15

not make the ordeal any more pleasant, but it gave her the necessary spinal fortitude. Not that there was anything wrong with the tea. There were scones and strawberry jam with cream obviously obtained from contented cows. There were *petit fours* in delightful colours and brandy snaps. There was Ceylon tea in the big silver teapot, and fine Chinese cups from which to drink it.

The only fly in the afternoon's ointment was Mrs William McNaughton. She was a pale, drooping woman, dressed in an unbecoming grey. Her sheaf of pale hair was coming adrift from its pins. These disadvantages could have been overcome with the correct choice of hairdresser and *couturière*, but the essential soppiness of her character was irreparable. Mrs William McNaughton reminded Phryne of jelly-cake and aspens and other quivering things, but there was steel under her flinching. This was a woman who had all the marks of extensive abuse: the hollow eyes, the nervous movements, the habit of starting at a sudden sound. But she had survived in her own way. She might cower, but she would not release hold of an idea once she had grasped it, and she could keep a secret or embark on a clandestine path. Her concealment of her character and

16

her desires would be close to absolute, and torture would not break her now if her past had not killed her. However, despite the reasons, Phryne could not like her. Phryne herself met all challenges head-on, and the Devil take the hindmost.

'It's my son, Miss Fisher,' said Mrs Mc-Naughton, handing Phryne a cup of tea. 'I'm worried about him.'

'Well, what worries you?' asked Phryne, pouring her cup of anaemic tea into the slop-bowl and filling it with a stronger brew. 'Have you spoken to him about it?'

'Oh, no!' Mrs McNaughton recoiled. Phryne added milk and sugar to her tea and stirred thoughtfully. The process of finding out what was bothering McNaughton was like extracting teeth from an uncooperative ox.

'Tell me, then, and perhaps I may be able to help,' she suggested.

'I have heard of your talents, Miss Fisher,' observed Mrs McNaughton artlessly. 'I hoped that you might be able to help me without causing a scandal. Lady Rose speaks very highly of you. She's a connection of my mother's, you know.'

'Indeed,' agreed Phryne, taking a brandy snap and smiling. Lady Rose had mislaid her emerald earrings, and was positive that her maid of long standing had not stolen them, thus contradicting her greedy nephew and heir, as well as the local policeman. She had hired Phryne to find the earrings, and this Phryne had done in one afternoon's inquiry amongst the local *Montes de Piété*, where the nephew had pawned them. He had made an unwise investment in the fourth at Flemington, putting the proceeds on a horse which was possessed of insufficient zeal and had not been able to redeem them. Lady Rose had been less than generous with the fee, but more than generous with her recommendations. Since Phryne did not need the money, she was pleased with the bargain. Lady Rose had told her immediate acquaintance that, 'She may look like a flapper – she smokes cigarettes and drinks cocktails and I believe that she can fly an aeroplane – but she has brains and bottom and I thoroughly approve of her.'

Since she had made the decision to become an investigator, Phryne had not been out of work. She had found the Persian kitten for which the little son of the Spanish ambassador was pining. It had been seduced by the delights of the nearby fish-shop's storehouse, and had been shut in. Phryne had released it, and (after it had suffered three baths) it was restored to its doting admirer. She had worked three weeks in an office, watching a costing clerk skimming the warehouse and blaming the shortfall on the inefficiency of a female stores clerk. Phryne had taken a certain delight in catching that one. She had watched a brutal and violent husband for long enough to obtain sufficient evidence for his battered wife to divorce him. For, in addition to her bruises and broken fingers, she needed to prove adultery. Phryne, who never shrank from a little bending of the rules, had provided the adulterer with a suitable partner from among the working girls of her acquaintance, and had paid the photographer's fee out of her own bounty. The husband was informed that the negatives would be handed over after the delivery of the decree absolute, and everyone wondered that such a determined and hard man went through his divorce like a lamb. His divorced wife was in possession of a comfortable competence and was reported to be very happy.

The result of all this work was that Phryne, to her surprise, was busy and occupied and had not been bored for months. She considered that she had found her *métier*.

Physically, Phryne had been described by the redoubtable Lady Rose as 'small, thin, with black hair cut in what I am told is a bob, disconcerting grey-green eyes and porcelain skin. Looks like a Dutch doll'. Phryne admitted this was a fair depiction.

For the interview with Mrs McNaughton, she had selected a beige dress of mannish cut, which she felt made her look like the directress of a women's prison, and matching taupe shoes and stockings. Her cloche hat was of a quiet dusty pink felt.

She was not getting anywhere with Mrs McNaughton, who had sounded frantic on the phone, but who now seemed unable to get to the point.

Phryne bit into the brandy snap and waited. Mrs McNaughton (who had not asked Phryne to call her Frieda) took a gulp of her watery tea and finally blurted out what was on her mind.

'I'm afraid my son is going to kill my husband!'

Phryne swallowed her brandy snap with some difficulty. This was not what she had been expecting.

'Why do you think that?' asked Phryne, calmly.

Mrs McNaughton felt inside her large

knitting bag, which had reposed on the sofa beside her and handed Phryne a crumpled letter. It looked like it had been retrieved from the fire, for it was singed at one edge.

Phryne unfolded it carefully, as the paper was brittle.

'If the pater doesn't come to the party, it will be all up,' she read aloud. 'Might have to remove him. Anyway, I am going to talk to him about it tonight, so wish me luck, kid.' It was signed, 'Yours as ever, Bill.'

'You see?' whispered Mrs McNaughton. 'He means to kill William. What am I to do?'

'Where did you find this?' asked Phryne. 'In the grate, was it?'

'Yes, how clever of you, Miss Fisher. My maid found it this morning when she was doing the rooms, it's a carbon copy. Bill always keeps carbons of his letters. He's so business like. He made a special arrangement to talk to William in the study tonight about this new venture, and I,' Mrs McNaughton's voice wavered, 'don't know what to do.'

'Remove could have other meanings than murder, Mrs McNaughton. What sort of venture?'

'Something to do with aeroplanes. Bill is a pilot, you know, and has won all sorts of races and things. It's so worrying for a mother,

21

Miss Fisher, having him flying. Those planes don't look strong enough to stay up in the sky, and I don't really believe they can, you know, being heavier than the air. He conducts a school at Essendon, Miss Fisher, teaching people to fly. But he wants capital from William for a new venture.'

'And what is that?' asked Phryne, interested. She loved planes.

'They want to fly over the South Pole – apparently the North Pole is old hat. "No one has tried planes down here," he said to me. "It's no use staying on the ground. It's all ice and desert, but in the air we can cover miles in minutes." And he wants William to put money into it.'

'And your husband does not agree?'

'He won't do it. They've had some terrible fights about money. William put up the capital to start the flying school, and it hasn't been going well. He insisted that he be Chairman of Directors of the company, and he has all the books brought to him every month, then he calls Bill in and they have an awful argument about how the business is going. He was furious about the purchase of the new plane.'

'Why?'

'He says that a company with such a cash

problem can't extend on capital – at least I think that's what he said. I don't know any of these business terms, I'm afraid. They are both big, hot tempered men with strong opinions – they are very like each other – and they have been fighting since Bill was born, it seems,' said Mrs McNaughton with surprising shrewdness. 'Amelia escaped a lot of it because she's a girl, and William does not expect anything of girls. Anyway she's dabbling in art at the moment, and she's hardly ever here. She wanted an allowance to go and live in a studio, but William put his foot down about that. "No daughter of mine is going to live like a Bohemian," he said, and wouldn't give her any money, but she enrolled in the gallery school against his wishes and she only comes home to sleep. She's no trouble,' said Mrs McNaughton, dismissing her daughter with a wave of her tea-cup. 'But Bill clashes. He disagrees with William to his face. I don't think they'll ever get on, and they behave as though they hate one another. Nothing but noise and shouting and my nerves can't bear much more. I've already had to go to Daylesford for the waters. I'm afraid that Bill will lose his temper and … and … do what he threatened, Miss Fisher. Can't you do something?'

'What would you like me to do?'

'I don't know,' wailed Mrs McNaughton. 'Something!' It appeared that she had relied on Phryne to wave a magic wand. As her hostess appeared to be on the verge of the vapours, Phryne made haste to assent.

'Well, I'll try. Where is Bill now?'

'He'll be at the airfield, Miss Fisher. The Sky-High Flying School. It's the red hangar at Essendon. You can't miss it.'

'I'll go there now,' said Phryne, putting down her cup. 'And I don't think you have any reason to be really upset, Mrs McNaughton. I think "remove" means "remove him from the board of directors" not "remove him from this world". But I'll talk to Bill, anyway.'

'Oh, thank you, Miss Fisher,' said Mrs McNaughton, fumbling for her smelling salts.

Phryne started the Hispano-Suiza which was her pride and dearest possession and sped back to the Windsor Hotel. She had found a house and was moving out, and hoped that her new home would be as comfortable as the hotel. The Windsor had everything Phryne needed: style, comfort, and room service. She parked her car and

24

ran up the stairs.

'Dot, do you want to come for a ride in a plane?' called Phryne from the bathroom to her invaluable and devoted maid. Dot, who had come by way of attempted manslaughter into Phryne's service, was a conservative young woman who had so far resisted the temptation to bob her long brown hair. She was a slim plain girl and was wearing her favourite brown overall. Dot did not like the idea of the Hispano-Suiza and the thought of being bodily hauled through the firmament, which should contain only birds and angels, did not appeal to her. She went to the bathroom door with a leather flying jacket over her arm.

'No, Miss. I don't want a ride in a plane.'

'All right, 'fraidy cat, what are you doing this afternoon? Want to come and watch, or have you something interesting to do?'

'I'll come and watch, Miss, but just don't ask me to go up in one of them things. Here's your breeches, and the leather coat. What about a hat, Miss?'

'There should be a flying helmet in the big chest.' Phryne pulled on breeches, a warm jersey and boots, then rummaged in the trunk, finally finding what looked like a battered leather bucket.

'Here we are. Take a coat, Dot, and come on. We have to go to Essendon to talk to Bill McNaughton. He's got a flying school. His mother thinks he's going to kill his father.'

Dot, inured to the shocking things that Phryne was prone to say, gathered up her blue winter coat and followed her employer down the stairs.

'And is he, Miss?'

'I don't know. The mother is the most nervous woman God ever put breath into. Both father and son sound like bruisers. However, we shall see. It's been too long since I was in a plane.'

The Hispano-Suiza roared into life. Phryne swung the big car out into traffic with efficient ease, and Dot closed her eyes, as she always did at the beginning of a journey in this car. It was so big, and so red and so noticeable, and Phryne's style of driving was so insolent and fast, that Dot found the whole equipage unladylike.

They covered the road to Essendon in little over half an hour and pulled to a stop near a red hangar. A neatly painted sign informed them that this was the 'Sky-High Flying School Pty Ltd, Prop: W. McNaughton'.

'Here we are, Dot, and off we go. This may

be a stormy interview, so stay on the edges of the crowd and be ready for a quick retreat.'

'Why difficult, Miss?'

'Well, you think of a delicate way to ask someone if they are going to kill their father.'

'Oh,' said Dot. She clutched her blue coat closer. It was a cold, clear afternoon, with little wind. Perfect, as Phryne saw, for flying. Three small planes were up, more or less, being flown by nervous, amateur hands. A bigger, faster two seater did a quick wing-wobble and dropped neatly, landing and running along the grassy strip with the minimum of bounce. The pilot taxied the machine to its resting place and climbed out, shouting at the top of his voice.

'A sweet little goer!' he enthused. 'Light on the controls, and just a bit nose heavy, but you warned me about that, Bill. Hello hello hello! Who's the lady?'

Phryne walked close enough to put out a hand, and shook the airman's gauntlet.

'I'm Phryne Fisher. I've done a little flying, but I haven't seen that 'bus before. What is it?'

'Fokker, a German company, made it. One of theirs flew the North Pole, mounted on skis. Jack Leonard, Miss Fisher. Glad to meet you. This is Bill McNaughton. It's his plane.'

Phryne put out her hand and had it engulfed to the wrist by a large paw. Mrs McNaughton had not told her that Bill stood six feet high and was built like a brick wall. Phryne's eyes ran up the scaffolding of leather flying suit to reach a large and ugly face. He was blond, with curls like a Hereford bull and intense blue eyes. The face was redeemed by a friendly grin.

'Pleased to meet you, Miss Fisher. Done some flying?' The sceptical tone offended Phryne. She had two hundred solo hours and a taste for stunt flying. She was no amateur. Bill might need some convincing.

'Yes, just a little,' she said sweetly. 'Perhaps I can take one of the Moths?'

'I'll come up too, Miss Fisher,' he said condescendingly. 'Just to keep you company.'

Phryne smiled again and climbed into the Moth. It was a sturdy biplane, perfect for beginners. It could land and take off on a handkerchief and had a stalling speed of forty miles per hour. She pulled on her helmet, breathing in the bracing scent of aviation fuel and grease.

'Let her go, Jack,' she yelled over the fracturing roar of the engine. Jack Leonard swung the propellor. The Gypsy Moth trundled on her bicycle wheels along the grassy paddock and lifted intoxicatingly into the air. Take-off was Phryne's favourite moment: the heart-lifting jolt as gravity gave way under pressure and the earth let go of the plane.

She steered the Moth into a loose circle above the landing-field. She could see the Hispano-Suiza below, gleaming like a Christmas beetle, and the matchstick figures of Dot and Jack Leonard. Behind her Bill McNaughton yelled 'Not a bad take-off, Miss Fisher, what else can you do?'

Phryne pulled back on the joystick and the little machine gained height. She scanned the sky carefully. No one around. The last nervous would-be flier had landed. The air was empty, cloudless and still. She glanced over her shoulder long enough to see Bill's smug grin. Phryne decided the time had come to wipe the smile off his face and stabbed down haul on the ailerons.

With an agonized whine, the Moth began to spin. Phryne blinked under the goggles as the air tore past her face. Down came her heel on the cable, paralysing the nursemaid controls which Bill was attempting to operate.

Falling like a leaf, spilling the wind from her wings, the Moth pancaked down. To all observers she appeared out of control. Phryne, her heart in her mouth, waited until she could see the look of horror on Dot's face quite clearly before she threw the little plane into a forward roll, turning with the spin, and spiralled it back up into the sky. Bill swore breathlessly. She let the Moth find her controls again and turned back to smile her sweetest.

'Do you think that I can fly, Mr McNaughton?' she shouted against the wind. She saw him nod. Then she released the cable and said, 'If you can keep this steady at fifty miles an hour, I'll show you an interesting trick.'

Phryne was completely above herself with reckless delight.

'All right, fifty she is,' agreed Bill, taking control.

'Keep her wings quite flat,' yelled Phryne. The plane levelled out and was flying quite smoothly. Phryne seized a strut, hung on tight, and got one knee up onto the top wing. Before the astounded Bill could cry out, she had gained the upper surface and was walking calmly along the wing, while he delicately rolled the plane a little to compensate for her weight. Sweat ran down his forehead and into his eyes. She had reached the end of the wing. She turned to come back.

Phryne faced into the gale with delight. The wind was no worse than in a racing car and the wing of the Moth was laced with struts of a suitable size into which to wedge a toe. She waved at the group on the ground and walked slowly back, noting that the tilt was being beautifully handled by her pilot.

He may not be a nice man but he flies like an angel, she thought, hanging briefly by her hands six hundred feet above an unforgiving earth before she dropped into her cockpit again.

'Good flying,' she yelled at Bill, but he did not answer.

Phryne took the Moth down to a near-textbook landing and hopped out of the pilot's seat into an admiring crowd.

'By Jove, Miss Fisher, haven't you any nerves at all?' asked Jack Leonard, pumping her hand up and down. 'We must have a drink on this. Come into the mess, we shall make you a member.'

Dot, who had ceased to watch when Phryne had climbed out onto the wing, was being escorted into the hangar by an attentive young man who was promising her tea. Bill followed slowly, shaking his head.

Jack showed Phryne into a small room at the back of the hangar, which had a bar and a lot of bentwood chairs. The metal walls were hung with trophies and photographs of grinning airmen with terrific moustaches, as well as a grim picture of a biplane breaking up in the course of a loop-the-loop.

He procured her a whisky and soda and sat down to admire.

'Where did you learn to fly?' he asked, as Bill joined him with a large glass of neat brandy, which he swallowed in one gulp.

'In England,' said Phryne. 'I learned to fly in a Moth. Beautiful little planes. You can make them do anything.'

'So I saw. That spin didn't look very controlled from down here but I expect you knew exactly what you were doing, eh, Miss Fisher?' Jack enthused. Bill grunted.

'You are a born flyer, Miss Fisher. If you got the impression I thought otherwise, I apologize. I had my insides in a twist the whole time you were aloft on the wing. What a stunt! Why haven't I heard of you before? Would you like to do some exhibition flying for us?'

'Who is "us"?' asked Phryne, sipping her drink, and wondering when her hands and shins were going to thaw.

'The Sky-High Flying School. It's my company.'

'I see. Well, perhaps it could be arranged. Mr Leonard, could I trouble you to look after my maid? I think she's had a shock.'

She gave Jack Leonard a forty-watt smile and he moved over to speak to Dot, who looked pale and weak. Phryne seized her moment and stared Bill in the eye.

'I had tea with your mother this morning. She wants me to ask you not to kill your father,' she whispered, and the big face flamed crimson.

'What? You insolent bitch, what has my family to do with you?'

'Keep your hair on and your voice down. I don't think you are going to kill your father, and if you call me an insolent bitch again I'll break your arm.' She put a delicate hand on his right wrist. 'That arm. If you can't control that temper of yours you will get into trouble. Now listen. You are having some sort of meeting with your father tonight, are you not?'

The huge man nodded dumbly.

'All right, then. Your mother is so frightened by the loud and angry way you and your father conduct your affairs that she truly thinks you might kill the old man. Why not try peaceful means? Is all that sound and fury essential?'

'It isn't me,' protested Bill. 'It's him. He knows a lot about business but nothing about flying – he's scared to death in the air, he's only been up once – and he tries to lay down the law to me about flying and I get angry, then he gets angry and then...'

'And then your poor mother has to put up with a scene that shatters her nerves again.'

'Well, what business is it of yours, Miss Fisher?'

'I told you. Your mother called me in to stop you from killing your father. I'm an investigator. I don't think you are really meaning to assassinate the man, but I have to do something to earn my retainer. Perhaps you could conduct your arguments somewhere else, if that is how you have to carry on,' she suggested. 'Here, for instance. No neighbours near, and your mother need never know.'

'That might be an idea. Of course, the mater has never been strong, but I didn't know it was upsetting her all that much. Amelia was always saying that the mater flinched at every sound, but you can't believe Amelia.'

'Why not?'

Bill snorted and leaned forward to whisper.

'The girl's potty. Gone off to be an artist, joined the gallery school and talks of nothing but light and colour. I never pay any attention to her. She's not interested in flying. But you, Miss Fisher, you're different. I'll do what I can,' conceded Bill. 'I don't want the mater to worry.'

'That's handsome of you,' said Phryne ironically, and began to talk aeroplane shop.

An hour later she extracted Dot from the friendly attentions of Jack Leonard and drove back to the city, exhilarated by her adventure and satisfied that Bill would curb his anger when he met with his father that night.

'Have you seen Candida?' asked Molly Maldon, perplexed. There were times when the strain of coping with Candida and her father told on Molly. She was a small woman, fiery and logical, with a wild Celtic streak. Henry Maldon always said that her temper had come with her red hair.

Molly could cope with the baby Alexander, because he was not subtle and because he was very young, but Candida frequently reduced her to pulp. She was an honest child who did not scruple to lie like a trooper if it suited her. She was a delicate asthmatic with the strength of ten and the willpower of Attilla the Hun. She was a sweet, affectionate angel who had nearly bitten her baby brother's ear off. Candida was very intelligent, and had taught herself to read, but occasionally did things that were so stupid that Molly wondered if the child was touched. Candida's natural mother had died in an asylum and Molly had been known to comment, in moments of complete exasperation, that it was Candida who had driven her there.

Henry Maldon looked up from his navigation tables. He was a tall vague man, with blue eyes and weathered skin. He always seemed to be looking into far horizons. This meant that he had scattered Melbourne with his keys, wallets, hats, cigarette lighters and on one inexplicable occasion, both socks.

'Oh, Henry, do buck up. Where is Candida?'

'She was right there,' said Henry, dragging his mind away from the South Pole. 'Sitting on the floor reading the newspaper. She liked the treasures from Luxor, and I promised to help her make a pyramid out of blocks if she let me alone to finish my sums. Then she was quiet for ... good God, a whole hour ... and I never heard her go out.'

'She knows that she is not allowed to leave the garden,' said Molly. 'The first thing to do is to search the house. Wake up, Henry, do! I have a nasty feeling about this.' Henry, alert at last, rummaged his way through the ground floor of the small house which he had recently bought. It had been so complete a windfall that he was still not altogether sure that it had happened. Most of the belongings were still in boxes, and it was not difficult to scour the places where even a cunning and vindictive six year old might secrete herself.

'Try the roof,' suggested Molly.

There was a ring at the doorbell. Molly ran down the passage and snatched the door open.

'You bad, bad girl,' she said, and realized that the caller was looking rather puzzled. It was her husband's old crony, Jack Leonard.

'I say, Molly, what's afoot? Been through the wars?'

'Candida's missing!' exclaimed Molly, bursting into tears. 'The spanking I shall give the little madam when I find her, she won't sit down for a week. Oh, Jack did you come in a car?'

'Yes, got the old motor outside. Do you want me to look for her?'

'Oh, Jack, please. She's only a little girl and I'm worried. She could have been gone for an hour.'

'Cheer up, old thing, that kid is as tough as ... I mean,' amended Jack Leonard, seeing a furious light in Molly's eyes, 'she's clever, Candida is. She won't come to any harm. I'll have a scout about. I'll find her, never fret. I say, Henry, this is a nice house. Bought with the ... er ... proceeds, I expect?'

'Yes, with the new plane and the money in the trust fund for the kids, I'm nearly as broke as when it happened. Molly hasn't even had time to unpack all the new furniture and things yet, and the garden's not even planted. All right, Molly,' said Henry Maldon hastily, detecting signs of combustion in his red-headed spouse. 'We'll go out directly. Come on, Jack.'

'Saw the most amazing thing this morning,' commented Jack Leonard as he piloted the car out from the curb. 'This spiffing young woman turned up at Bill McNaughton's school and spun a Moth.'

'They will spin, if you mistreat 'em bad enough,' agreed Henry Maldon absently. He was beginning to wonder about Candida. Usually she was reliable, but she had a strange, wilful streak and might wander anywhere, if it struck her as a compellingly good idea. 'Amateur, was she?'

'No, old boy, an expert. It was a controlled spin down to three hundred feet, then she zoomed out of it, and all with good old Bill in the dickey. Then she upped and waltzed out onto the top wing and walked from one end to another. I tell you one thing, Henry, if I could find a woman like that, damned if I wouldn't marry her. But she wouldn't have me. Poor Bill, he was as white as a sheet when Miss Fisher finally let him take the crate down. Nearly kissed the runway. You aren't listening, are you, Henry?'

'No,' agreed Henry. 'I can't see her any-where.'

'Miss Fisher?'

'Candida!' he snapped. 'Drive round again, Jack, and do stop talking. I want to think.' Jack Leonard, although childless, did not take offence, and turned the car yet again.

CHAPTER TWO

To be poor and independent is very nearly
an impossibility
Advice to Young Men, William Cobbett

Phryne whisked Dot into town, taking St
Kilda Road at a sedate twenty miles an hour.

'Are you all right, old thing?' she called.
Dot, huddled into her blue coat, did not
answer. Phryne pulled up outside a small
house on The Esplanade, which was her new-
est acquisition, and turned off the engine.

'Dot?' she asked, shaking her maid by the
shoulder.

Dot turned on Phryne, her face still
blanched with shock.

'You nearly scared me to death, Miss.
When I saw you climb out of that machine
I thought ... I thought...' Phryne enveloped
Dot in a warm hug.

'Oh, dear Dot, you mustn't start worrying
about me. I'm sorry I scared you, my dear
old bean ... there, dry your eyes, now, and
don't concern yourself. I've done that trick

thousands of times, it's easy. Anyway, next time I do something like that, don't watch. All right? Now, have you got the keys? All the inside work should be finished, and the housekeeper should be here.'

Dot sniffed, pocketed her handkerchief and found the keys. She smiled shakily at Phryne who had leapt lightly out of the car and was waiting at the front gate.

It was a neat, bijou townhouse, faced with shining white stucco so that it looked like an iced cake. It had two storeys and a delightful attic room with a gable-window which Dot had claimed. She had never had a bedroom of her own until she had come to work for Phryne, and she still found the idea tantalizing. A room with a door which you could lock, a place to be completely alone until you wanted to let the world in.

Phryne stood aside in the little porch to allow Dot to open the front door, which was solid mahogany. The hall was dark, and Phryne had lightened it with white paint, upon which the stained glass fanlight cast beautiful colours. The ground level rooms, which as yet were sparsely furnished, were floored with bare polished boards and overlaid with fine Turkish rugs. In front of the large fireplace was a rug made of sheepskin, on which Phryne intended to recline. The decor was cool greens and gold, reflecting the timber floor, and there was only one painting; a full-length nude holding a jar out of which water was spilling, to fall in a cascade at her feet. It was called 'La Source' and it bore a striking resemblance to Phryne herself. Dot disliked this painting intensely.

Phryne called into the silent house 'Hello? Anyone here?' and in answer a stout woman in a wrapper fought her way through the bead curtain and said, 'Well, Miss Fisher, is it? I'm Mrs Butler. The agency sent me. Mr Butler is outside, dealing with the plumber'

'Phryne Fisher, and this is Miss Dorothy Williams, my personal maid and secretary. What's wrong with the plumbing?' asked Phryne, wearily, for she had spent weeks on the design of a luxurious bathroom and indoor WC and she was going to have them no matter what the plumber said. So far he had charged her twice his quoted price and she was minded to become quite harsh with him if the house was not entirely ready, with everything that was supposed to flush, flushing.

'Mr Butler is dealing with him, Miss. You'll find that it will all be ready tomorrow when you move in, just as you wish,' soothed Mrs Butler, with a hint of steel in her voice. If she cooked as well as he managed plumbers, Mr and Mrs Butler were going to be a find.

'Now, what about a cup of tea, Miss? I've got the kettle on, and perhaps you'd like to see the kitchen, now that it is all finished?'

'Yes, I would, thank you, we've had a tiring day, eh, Dot? And more shocks than are good for us, perhaps.'

Dot followed Phryne through the bead curtain into the kitchen. It was a big room, with a red brick floor and new green gas stove on legs. There were two sinks, newly installed, and a hot-water heater with a permanent flame. Phryne's new dishes had all been washed and stacked in an old pine dresser, and the window was open onto her neat backyard, with garden furniture and a fernery. The despised outdoor lavatory was newly scrubbed and painted for the use of the domestics.

Mrs Butler tipped boiling water into the teapot and set it down. Phryne took a chair.

'Well, it all looks nice. How do you think you'll like it here, Mrs Butler? Is there anything you need?'

'Not so far, Miss. The tradesmen call every morning, and all the appliances work. Nice to have a gas stove. An Aga stove is warm in the winter, and there's nothing better for bread, but it's a trial in the summer, to be sure. And the electrical fires are lit, and the real ones, Miss. The house will warm up in a few hours. It will be ready for you tomorrow, with luncheon on the table. Will you be dining in?'

'Yes. I haven't much on hand at the moment. How about your room, Mrs Butler? I thought that you would rather bring your own things.'

'Yes, Miss, it's fine. Nice view over the yard, and my suite fits in perfect. I'm sure we'll be very happy here. Your tea, Miss.'

Phryne drank her tea, and paid attention to the raised voices in the yard. Mr Butler and the plumber appeared to be exchanging hearty curses. Phryne noticed that Dot still looked rather pinched and suggested, 'Come up and have a look at your room, Dot. You'll want to see how the furniture fits in. Thanks for the tea, Mrs B. I hope we'll be here about eleven tomorrow.'

Dot raced up the stairs to the first floor, where Phryne had a bedroom in moss green and a sitting-room in marine tones. She opened the door to her own little stair. It was carpeted with brown felt, had an enchanting twist in the middle and led into the attic room.

Because it was at the top of the house it was always warm, and Dot, who had been chilled to the bone since early childhood, luxuriated in heat. She had chosen the furniture herself: a plain bed, wardrobe and dressing-table, a washstand and jug, and a table and padded chair by the window. It was all painted in Dot's favourite collection of colours; oranges and beiges and browns. Covering her bed was a bedspread made of thousands of velvet autumn leaves. Dot sank down on it with delight.

'I saw it in the market, and thought that you'd like it,' said Phryne's voice behind her. 'Here are your keys, Dot. This is the room and this is the door at the bottom of your stair. I've got a spare pair and Mrs Butler has them in her bunch so she can clean, but otherwise you are on your own. I'll just go and look at my bed-hangings.' Phryne went out, closing the door behind her.

Dot rubbed her face on the velvet, then smoothed it into place again. Of all presents she had been given in her short life, and they had not been many, this was the best. This space was hers alone. No one else had any rights in it. She could put something down and it would remain there. She could lock her door and no one had a right to make her unlock it. Her mistress might be vain, promiscuous, and vague, not to mention prone to frightening Dot to death, but she had given Dot a great gift and had sufficient tact to go away and let her enjoy it. Dot sat in her padded chair, stared out to sea and loved Phryne from her heart.

Phryne inspected her bed-hangings, which were black silk embroidered with green leaves, and her mossy sheets, which were dark to show off her white body. Her carpet was green and soft as new grass, and her mirrors appropriately pink, and framed in ceramic vine leaves. All she needed now was a bacchanalian lover to match the room.

She smiled as she surveyed her male acquaintance. No one leapt to mind. However, something would come along. She might leave it for awhile until she found out how her staff would react. She had yet to meet the plumber-conquering Mr Butler. Phryne calculated that she had given Dot enough time to enjoy her room and called softly, 'Dot? Let's go and have dinner, or would you like to stay? You can come along in the morning, and help me pack.'

Phryne did not hear the feet on the stairs,

but Dot's voice was close. 'Oh, can I stay, Miss?'

'Certainly. Come to the hotel at about eight, though. We've got a lot to do.'

'Oh, yes, Miss,' breathed Dot.

Phryne collected her coat and drove back to the city. She telephoned a flying friend she knew from her schooldays, and asked her to dinner, to re-acquaint herself with the aeroplane world.

'Bunji' Ross was a bracing young woman with an Eton crop and shoulders like a wrestler. She had begun life as a track rider, but had been discovered to be female and thrown out of the stables. She had no chance of becoming a jockey as she was too tall and heavy but found that the same qualifications that had made her a good rider made her a good flier. She had sharp reflexes, strong hands and most importantly, she never panicked.

'Of course, Phryne, you never met Ruth Law, did you?' asked Bunji, as she sat down in the Windsor's plush dining-room and stared hopelessly at the menu. 'I say, old girl, I don't really go for all this stuff, you know. I suppose steak and chips is out of the question?'

'Steak and chips you shall have, Bunji, old

bean,' agreed Phryne, turning to the waiter. *'Filet mignon and pommes frites* for Madame, and bring me lobster mayonnaise. Champagne,' she added to the hovering wine waiter. 'The Widow '23. No, I didn't meet Ruth Law, what was she like?'

'A charming woman, and a simply ripping flier. But she was involved in a bad crash and her husband had a *crise de nerfs* and begged her not to fly again. As far as I know she hasn't. Terrible waste. I hear you did a Perils of Pauline on a Moth, Phryne.'

'News travels fast out here.'

'Well, everyone knows everyone in the flying fraternity. Mostly it is a fraternity, too, only a few other females in Melbourne. But there's more coming up, you know. I've got six in my class at the moment; good girls, too. Like I always say, all you need for flying is good reflexes and light hands. You don't need brute force. In fact brute force will crash you nine times out of ten. Trouble is the cost of a 'bus. Look at Bill McNaughton, he's just spent a small fortune on a new Fokker, and what is he going to do with it? Fly over the South Pole, by all that's crazy.'

'I met him,' said Phryne, as the waiter filled her glass.

'Did you?'

'Yes, he was flying the Moth while I did my stunt.'

'You're a braver woman than me, then.'

'Why, what's wrong with him?'

'Brute force, like I say. Wrenches his machine around as if there were no such things as metal fatigue and tensile strengths. Saw him rip the wings off a Moth once, and that takes doing. You know how forgiving they are, nicest little things, apart from a tendency to buck – a child could fly them. But Bill has never learned that muscle ain't the solution to every problem. That's what's wrong with him.'

'I told him to keep her to a steady path and compensate for the tilt, and he did.'

'Well, that's more than I would have thought of him. I wouldn't try it. He'd be just as likely to loop the loop with you aloft. I'd say you had a lucky escape, old girl. Let me fill up your glass. You look pale.'

'I feel pale,' agreed Phryne. 'What do you know about him, then?'

'Bill? His father stumped up manfully for him to start his flying school. It ain't going well. He's a lousy teacher. Yells at his pupils and frightens them into fits, then won't let them try on their own. They either give up flying or come to me. I've had three of his ex-pupils. He'd reduced all of them to pulp, especially the men. He doesn't really think that women can fly, so he's not so hard on 'em. It don't do a young man any harm to be pulped occasionally. Stop 'em from getting above 'emselves. However, you can't expect them to pay for it. He's a bruising flier – brave but brash, and he breaks his machines. Luckily, he's a good mechanic so he can repair his own. Word is that he gets on very badly with his dad, which is not surprising, because they are much alike. Both big, loud, self-opinionated bastards. This steak is jolly good,' added Bunji, and tucked in joyfully. Phyrne picked at her lobster mayonnaise and sipped champagne. She was obscurely worried about Bill McNaughton. Having intruded into his life, she now felt responsible for him.

'Why not fly over the South Pole?' she asked, idly.

'Too big,' said Bunji with her mouth full. 'The North Pole is big, but most of it is ice, and so when some of the ice melts there's a lot less land to cross. The South Pole, I believe is mostly land overlaid with ice and when the ice melts it ain't going to get any smaller. And ice does funny things to planes. Look at poor old Nobile, the Italian, who took the airship over the North Pole. The planes sent out to rescue him all crashed, either on landing or on taking off again. That Fokker of McNaughton's was one of the planes they sent out after him, and it only managed one journey before it crashed, nose heavy in icy air. Nothing can carry enough fuel to stay up all the way over, that's the problem. If we could refuel in mid-air it would be different. Without a working radio and a few new inventions, it ain't possible, Phryne. And I'm the woman who flew the Pyrenees in January. I know about snow. What shall we have for dessert? And can you lend me a gown, Phryne? I've got to go to a ball, to get a prize for that speed event, and they won't let me wear my flying togs.'

Phryne sighed, as every dress she had ever lent Bunji had come back ruined; but she smiled, suggested trifle for dessert, and agreed. After all, considering her childhood of miserable poverty, it was nice to have so many dresses that it did not matter that one of them was ruined. She ate her trifle, reflecting that grinding poverty, though loathsome while one is in it, has the advantage of making one enjoy money in a way denied to the rich-from-birth.

It also enabled one to fulfil one's sillier impulses. She reached into her bag and gave Bunji her newly printed card.

'Miss Phryne Fisher. Investigations. 221B, The Esplanade, St Kilda,' read Bunji. 'You becoming a private Dick, eh? What larks! And what luck about the address.'

'It wasn't luck, I just added a B to 221. I bought the house for the number. You must drop in and see me, Bunji. Now come upstairs and we'll find you a gown.'

Luckily, none of Phryne's favourite gowns would fit the chunky Bunji, who was satisfied with a plain, loose artist's smock in dark velvet which Phryne had bought on a whim and had never worn.

'No, I don't want it back. I never liked it, and it suits you beautifully. How about a hat?'

Bunji chose an extravagant felt with a bunch of violets over one ear in which she looked indescribable. Phryne did not shudder but packed it up in a box and rang for tea.

'By the way, there's a daughter in that family – Amelia, I think that's her name. She came to watch Bill fly once. Arty type. Grubby but pretty, slender and pale. I asked her if she wanted to go up with me and she came over all faint, had to be helped to a chair,' Bunji snorted, not unkindly.

'Poor kid, living with them two, she's had all the spirit crushed out of her. But she did a fine watercolour of the flight. Don't know anything about art but I thought she was rather good. She gave it to me, and I put it on the wall at once. Bill saw it and said, "It's very nice of you to encourage my sister, Bunji," as if the stuff was rubbish, and I came right back at him and said that I thought it was a jolly good painting and that he was a Philistine, but by then the girl had crept away. He's a brute, Bill is. I don't like him. Anyway, dear, ta for the tea and the dinner, and thanks for the gown. I'll come and see you when you're settled, Sherlock, and if you want a bit of a fly, just look me up.'

Bunji breezed off, and Phryne, rather depressed, put herself to bed.

CHAPTER THREE

'Qu'ils mangent de la brioche'
('Let them eat cake')
Marie Antionette (attributed)

Dot sat down to an early tea with Mr and Mrs Butler. There was thick vegetable soup, an egg-and-bacon pie, and apple crumble, with many cups of strong kitchen tea.

'Well, Else, I reckon it's a nice little house and she's a nice girl, eh?' beamed Mr Butler, who had won his duel with the plumber. Everything that Miss Fisher had decreed should flush, now flushed enthusiastically, and the electric fires about which Mr Butler had had doubts, were working perfectly. Dot frowned. She did not know if this was a correct way to speak about Phryne.

'She's a lady,' reproved Mrs Butler. 'And don't you forget it, Ted. She's got grand relations at Home and her dad is related to the King.'

'She's still a nice girl. Knows what she

wants and gets it. And pays for it. Us, for instance.'

'You see, my dear,' Mrs B. said to Dot, 'we weren't going to take another place when our old gentleman died. Such a nice man. He had good connections, too. He left us enough money to retire – a little house in Richmond and a bit of garden, just what we've always wanted. But Ted and me, we ain't old yet and somehow we didn't really want to retire, not if we could find a good place. A smaller establishment, with no children and other help coming in for the laundry and the rough work. We put ourselves on the books of the most exclusive agency, and doubled our wages. Miss Fisher sent the solicitor to interview us and we told the lawyer what we wanted. All Miss Fisher required was that we swore not to disclose any of her personal affairs to anyone, and naturally we'd never do that. Then the solicitor upped and asked us when we could move in to supervise the alterations, and so we agreed to try out for six months and see if we suited one another. So far it's going well. What about you, dear?'

'I've been with her for three months,' replied Dot. 'She helped me out of a scrape. I was out of place because the son of the house was chasing me, and she took me on. Since we started this private investigator stuff it's been all go. The only thing that might annoy you is tea at all hours if she's working on a problem, otherwise she's lovely,' said Dot, taking another mouthful of apple crumble. 'This is delicious,' she added. Mrs Butler smiled. Like all good cooks, she loved feeding people.

'Do you like cars, Mr Butler?' Dot asked.

'Call me Ted. I love cars. Always wanted to handle a machine like Miss Fisher's. Lagonda, is it?'

'Hispano-Suiza,' corrected Dot. 'She drives like a demon.'

Ted's eyes lit up. 'I expect she'll let me drive her to parties and balls and so on. I shall have to get a chauffeur's cap.'

Dot wondered how she was to mention Phryne's habit of strewing her boudoir with beautiful naked young men. She could not think of a method of introducing the subject and decided to leave it to Phryne to cope with.

'Well, Miss Williams, the bath water's hot if you want it,' said Mr Butler. 'And the whatsername works, at last. I'm going to polish the silver,' he said, and took himself off into the back of the house.

'Call me Dot. I've got to be at the hotel by eight, Mrs Butler, so can you manage some breakfast at seven? Just tea and toast. Good night.'

Dot climbed the stairs to her own room, washed her face and hands, and fell into a dreamless sleep in her own bed, in her own room. Outside the sea roared in the first of the winter's storms, but in 221B The Esplanade Dot was as snug as a bug in a rug.

Breakfast the next morning was bacon and eggs. Mrs Butler exclaimed at the idea of sending such a thin young woman out for a long day's work on tea and toast. Unusually full, Dot caught the tram and arrived at the Windsor in a lowering chill. The wind had dropped but the sky was full of rain. Dot clutched her coat close and ran up the steps, greeting the doorman as she passed.

'You must be freezing!' she exclaimed, as he fumbled with the big door.

'Not as bad yet as it's going to be,' he opined, cocking a knowing eye at the sky. 'Miss Fisher ain't going to walk any aeroplanes today.'

Dot found Phryne dropping her third armload of dresses onto her bed and staring at them.

'I had no idea that I had this many clothes,

Dot. I should give them away, what a collection.'

'No, you need them all, Miss. You sit down and I'll start packing. You make out a cheque for the bill, and I'll have this all put away in a jiffy. By the way, the doorman knew about your stunt in the plane. You must be in the paper.'

'Oh, good I'll go down and buy one. Can you cope?'

Dot nodded. She would cope much better if Phryne was not there. Phryne took her cheque book and bag and went out to drink coffee in the morning room and check each item in a voluminous bill. She was sorry to leave the Windsor. In it she had found great joy with her lover, Sasha of the *Compagnie des Ballets Masques,* now returned to France. While staying here she had broken a cocaine ring and had been instrumental in catching a notorious abortionist. It had been a fascinating three months but one could not live in a hotel all one's life. She sighed and poured more coffee. A bottle of Benedictine? When had she ordered that?

Left alone, Dot packed away all of the clothes, the shoes and hats and multitudinous undergarments and cosmetics and books and papers. She counted the jewellery into its

58

casket, locked it and pocketed the key. Then she rang the bell for the minions and went downstairs to see if Bert and Cec had arrived to carry the luggage.

Offending the Windsor's sacred precincts stood Bert, in deep conversation with the doorman. Bert was short and stout. He had curly brown hair and a hand-rolled cigarette firmly glued to his lower lip. His mate Cec, lanky and blonde, stood guarding a dreadful van at the foot of the steps. Traffic edged around it, hooting bitterly.

Phryne made three corrections in the bill, added it up anew, wrote out a cheque for a truly staggering amount and summoned the manager. He came with a long tail of staff members behind him, each wishing to be remembered by Miss Fisher.

Her pile of luggage was being carried out by Bert, Cec and several boys who wished to acquire merit. Phryne rewarded them all, beginning with the smallest boy, and working her way up to the august Manager himself, to whom she handed a sizeable *douceur*, which he took without a flicker.

'Goodbye,' said Phryne, giving him her hand. 'I really hate to leave you, but there it is. Thank you so much,' she smiled upon the enriched and grateful, and walked out of the

Windsor, trailing her clouds of glory.

She took her seat in the Hispano-Suiza, making the journey quickly, for it was freezing in the open car, despite her furs. She pulled up in style to meet Mr Butler at the gate. Dot preferred to travel with Bert and Cec.

'Just bring her in here, Miss, and mind the paintwork. Nicely she goes,' he instructed, and Phryne took the car in without mishap.

Mr Butler grinned and passed a doting hand over the red bonnet.

'Mr Butler, I presume? Do you like the car?'

'That I do, Miss She's a beauty.'

'Good. See if you can get the hood up, I'm frozen. Winter seems to have come, eh? I'm expecting you to drive this car for me, so you can take her out for a little practice later, if you like. But be careful of her, she's the only one in Australia, and where we shall get parts for her I do not know. I must go in, my toes have gone numb,' were Phryne's parting words before she ran up the garden path to the back door.

She walked into a wave of warmth and the scent of cooking and dropped into a chair in the sitting-room, where there was a small bright fire. Mrs Butler bustled in.

'Tea, Miss? Are you cold?'

'Frozen, but rapidly thawing. Coffee might be better, but you'll need to make tea for Bert and Cec and Dot, who are coming with the luggage.'

'Very good, Miss. Cutlets for lunch, with creamed potatoes? Apple pie for dessert?'

Phryne nodded, and took off one shoe. Her toes really had gone numb. She rubbed them briskly, reflecting that the Melbourne winter looked like being long and trying. She was grateful for the fire and all her other blessings for a quiet five minutes, before there was a thump at the door and she knew that the luggage had arrived.

Bert and Cec were a team. They had worked together for so long, in the army and on the wharf, that each seemed to sense where the other was. Consequently they were very efficient.

Apart from a few loud comments on her decor, Phryne did not hear a word or a bump as her possessions were carried up the stairs with ease and despatch.

'Come and have tea,' Phryne shouted as the last chest was carried in and Dot shut the doors of the sagging van.

Mrs Butler brought in a trolley laden with cakes and sandwiches, and the big kitchen teapot. Bert and Cec clumped down the stairs to accept cups and perch themselves on the over-stuffed chairs.

'How have things been going?' she asked, and Bert grinned.

'We bought a bonzer new taxi,' he took a sandwich, 'and we sold the old grid. It's been going good, Miss. And you're in the paper, did you see?' he added, flourishing the early *Herald*. Phryne looked at the front page. Bert's stubby finger pointed out a picture of a young woman poised on the upper wing of a biplane, with the legend 'The Hon. Phryne Fisher in Flight' then her eyes dropped to a stop press underneath.

'Mr William McNaughton was found dead on his tennis court today from head injuries. Police inquiries are continuing.'

'Oh, Bert, look at that,' she whispered.

Bert read the paragraph and said, 'Yair? Another capitalist bites the dust. So what?'

'His wife is a client of mine. Are you on, if I need you?' Bert handed Cec a cake and took one himself.

'Yair, Cec and me is on,' he agreed. 'Good cakes these.'

Dot finished her tea and ran lightly up the stairs to begin unpacking. Mr Butler accompanied her, more ponderously, with a pinch bar to open the tea-chests. Phryne wondered whether she should ring Mrs McNaughton, while Bert read another part of the paper aloud.

'Irish Lottery won by Melbourne Flyer,' he said. 'Blimey! What a bloke could do with ten thousand quid.'

'Really?' asked Phryne. 'What bloke is that?'

'It's here, in yesterday's *Herald*. Henry Maldon, famous flyer, who last year won the air race from Sydney to Brisbane, has been confirmed as the winner of the Irish Christmas Lottery, a sum exceeding ten thousand pounds sterling. Mr Maldon today refused to either confirm or deny that he was the winner, but his housemaid Elsie Skinner agreed the letter bearing the superscription "Irish Lottery" had arrived on that Monday in January, and that both Mr and Mrs Maldon seemed very happy. Mr Maldon has been married for three years to the former Miss Molly Hunter, the daughter of a prominent grazier family. They have one child, Alexander. The six-year-old child of Mr Maldon's former marriage, Candida, lives with the family. When asked what he would do with the money, Mr Maldon closed the door and refused to talk to our reporter.'

'I don't blame him,' commented Phryne.

'Yair, and I can think of one housemaid who is now out of a job,' said Bert.

'Yes. Will you stay for lunch?' asked Phryne, and Bert shook his head.

'We got a living to make,' he said gloomily, then spoiled the effect by grinning. 'So give us a shout if we can help with any of the ... er ... rough work, Miss.'

He collected Cec and departed. Phryne took up the newspaper and began to read. She was restless and could not concentrate. How had Mr McNaughton died? Had Bill been arrested? Should she call Mrs McNaughton, who would be a bundle of hysterics by now?

Phryne was summoned by Dot, who wanted her to make the final decision on which of her clothes were to be given away, and the subject proved so absorbing that lunch was announced before the two of them had finished more than half of the garments.

The cutlets, creamed potato and peas and the apple pie were excellent, and Phryne said so, treating herself to two cups of coffee before she allowed Dot to drag her back to her room. After another hour, Dot had stored all the good clothes and had a heap of rejects in the middle of the floor.

Phryne stood up and said decisively, 'You can have whatever you like, Dot, and then you have my full permission to dispose of the rest. I am going to ring Mrs McNaughton. I should have done so before, but she is going to be in such a state...

At that moment, the doorbell rang, and Phryne heard Mr Butler's firm tread in the hall. There was the sound of the door opening, then a faint shriek and a thud. Phryne ran down the stairs and encountered Mr B. carrying a limp bundle with some difficulty.

'Mrs McNaughton, Miss,' he observed gravely.

'Lay her on the couch, please, and ask Mrs B. for some tea.' Phryne removed the woman's hat and elevated her feet. Dot produced smelling salts.

'They've arrested Bill,' whispered Mrs McNaughton, and lapsed back into unconsciousness.

Mrs McNaughton had not been treated well by the stresses inherent in having a murdered husband and a murderous son. Her face was puffy with long crying and her fair hair straggled all down her unmatching dress and coat. As Phryne eased her into a more comfortable position, three soaked handkerchiefs fell out of her sleeve.

'Poor woman,' observed Phryne. 'I think we need a doctor, Dot. See if there's a local one. Mrs B. might know. Tell him we can pick him up if he hasn't got any transport. Ask Mr B. to ring the lady's house and tell her staff that she is here, in case they are worried about her. And I shall fetch a blanket,' she added to the empty room. She found a soft grey blanket in the linen closet and wrapped Mrs McNaughton carefully, as she, was now shivering. She sat down on her new easy chair and began to search her patient's handbag.

There were keys, more wet hankies, salts, powder compact, a search warrant for the house, telephone number of Russell Street's Police Station, one fountain pen (leaking), Phryne's card, a card-case (mother-of-pearl), two letters tied with ribbon, a purse with seven pound three and eight-pence, and some powders in paper, marked 'Mrs McNaughton. One powder as required'.

Phryne replaced all the chattels except the letters and opened them carefully, sliding off the elaborate bow of ribbon. She read rapidly, with one eye on her inert client, who moaned occasionally. As she read, her eyebrows rose until they disappeared under

66

her bangs.

'A fine robust turn of phrase the gentleman has,' she commented aloud. 'Who is he?' She leafed through the pages of passionate prose and found the signature. 'Your devoted Gerald'. Gerald had not carried his frankness as far as putting his full name or address on the letters. Phryne folded them carefully in their original creases and slipped them back into the envelopes and the ribbon. Mrs McNaughton had hidden depths. Her husband's name was – or had been – William and she had been married for many years. The letters were recent, the paper and ink were fresh. The incriminating correspondence was back in the bag and Phryne was staring idly into the fire by the time Dot and Mr B. re-entered, escorting a very young doctor.

He was tall and slim, with curly hair and dark brown eyes. Phryne felt an immediate interest and stood up to greet him. He took a stride forward, caught his foot in the hearthrug, and almost fell into Phryne's arms. She embraced him heartily, feeling the strong flat muscles in his back before she replaced him on his feet and smiled at him.

'I'm Phryne Fisher,' she said warmly. 'Are you the local doctor?'

'Yes,' stammered the enchanting young

man, blushing with embarrassment. 'Sorry. I still haven't got used to the length of my legs. Hope I didn't hurt you. I'm Dr Fielding. I've just started with old Dr Dorset, I've only been here a few months.'

'I've just moved in,' said Phryne. 'I hope we shall be friends. Meanwhile, this is Mrs McNaughton.' She indicated the supine woman, and Dr Fielding lost his clumsiness. He took a chair and sat down beside the patient, gestured to Mr B. to bring his bag, then gently pulled back the ragged hair from her face. He unhooked his watch and took her pulse, put away the watch, and laid the limp hot hand down carefully.

'She's collapsed from some terrible shock,' he said sternly. 'What has happened?'

'Her son has just been arrested for murdering her husband,' said Phryne. 'I think that you would call that a terrible shock. She arrived at the door in a state and fainted into Mr B.'s arms. Did she say anything, Mr Butler?'

'No, Miss Fisher. Just her name. Then she keeled over. Shall I fetch anything, Doctor?' His voice was quietly respectful.

'Yes, can you go down to the chemist and fill this prescription,' Dr Fielding scribbled busily. 'I can give her an injection which will help for the moment, and then she should be put to bed.'

'Doctor, she doesn't live here,' protested Phryne. 'She should be taken to her own home. And if I am to investigate the matter, I need her awake, at least for a short time, to tell me what happened when her husband was murdered.' Dr Fielding looked Phryne in the eye.

'I will not give the patient anything that will act to her detriment, Miss Fisher.'

'I am not asking you to, Dr Fielding. All I want is a safe stimulant so that she can tell me what she wants me to do. I can't act without instructions, and only she can give them to me. If she's going to be laid up with an attack of brain fever or something she might be *non compos* for weeks.' Dr Fielding compressed his lips, shook his head, counted the pulse again, then filled a syringe with a clear liquid. He gave the injection, then sat down again, watching his patient's face attentively.

Mrs McNaughton stirred and tried to sit up. Phryne brought a glass of water, and she sipped.

'Oh, Miss Fisher, you must help me. They've arrested Bill.'

'Delighted to help, but you must calm

down, take a deep breath, and tell me what happened.'

'I went out to call in Danny the dog. It was getting dark and I heard him howling, on the tennis-court. I went out and there was William lying on the court with his head ... horrible, all that blood ... and I screamed, and the police came, and took Bill away and now they'll hang him.'

Her voice was rising into hysteria. Dr Fielding put a large soothing hand on her wrist. Phryne smiled as confidently as she could.

'Calm yourself, my dear. I will investigate the matter. Today I'll go and see Bill and I'll do my best to get him out. All you have to do is close your eyes and rest. You won't be useful to Bill in your present state. Now Dr Fielding will give you an injection and when you wake up you'll be in your own house.'

Dr Fielding was prompt upon his cue and the tortured eyes lost their rigid gaze.

'Right, now we shall see what we shall see. Mr B., what about the medicine?'

'I've sent the boy next door for it, Miss. I thought that I should call Mrs McNaughton's home.'

'Quite right. Was anyone home?'

'Yes, Miss, the lady's daughter. She is on

70

her way to fetch her mother and asks that we wait for her. She has also given me the name and telephone number of the lady's own medical practitioner. I've telephoned him and he would like a word with Dr Fielding.'

Dr Fielding paled, tripped over a small table, and took the receiver. There was a short conversation which Phryne did not catch, then he hung up. A relieved smile illuminated his pleasant face.

'I appear to have adopted the right course of treatment. Her doctor says that she is a nervous subject. Well, you don't need me any more, Miss Fisher.'

'Oh yes I do,' said Phryne hurriedly, unwilling to let the first pretty young man she had seen for weeks out of her sight. 'Please stay until the daughter comes and oversee the start of the journey, at least. Sit down, Doctor. We shall have tea.'

Dr Fielding was a skilled medical practitioner, but his social encounters had been limited. Against Phryne he did not stand a chance.

He sat down and accepted a cup of tea.

Molly Maldon received the return of Jack Leonard and her husband with barely-concealed anxiety.

'Nothing?' she whispered. Henry shook his head.

'She was angry with me for not taking her to the lolly shop,' Mrs Maldon sat down suddenly. 'She stopped asking me, after a while, and that isn't like Candida. The lolly shop. Of course!' Without taking off her apron or putting on her hat, Molly Maldon ran down the hall and out through the door, into the street like a steeplechaser. Jack and Henry looked at each other, and shook their heads. There was no accounting for women. It was well-known.

Molly tore round the corner and struggled through the bamboo curtain. The window was packed with gingerbread men in golden coats. How Candida had coveted those sixpenny gingerbread soldiers. After her spanking she should have a whole one to herself, thought Molly. The shop bell jangled wildly.

'Have you seen a small girl in a blue dress, fair hair, and an Alice band?'

'Why yes,' said the shopkeeper. 'She told me her name – Candida, she said. Spent threepence on lollies. I told her not to eat them all at once. Why? Ain't her dad brought her home yet? He left a good two hours ago.'

'Her dad?' gasped Molly, wondering for a distracted moment if Henry were playing a joke on her. If so, he would know how she felt about it seconds after he gave Candida back.

'Yes, in a big black car, a woman and a man.'

'What kind of car?'

'Like I said, a big black one. My Jimmy might have noticed more, clean mad about motors, he is.'

'Where is Jimmy, then?'

'He's gone to school, Missus, he was only here for lunch, but he'll be home at half-past three, if you want to come back. What's the trouble? Has something happened to the little girl?'

'Yes,' said Molly, and ran out of the shop.

There, lying in the gutter, was a bag of sweets. Mint leaves and silver sticks spilled onto the ground. Molly gathered them up tenderly and ran back to her husband.

'Hello, old girl, did you find her?' asked Henry, looking up from the depths of a comfortable armchair. Molly flung the bag of lollies into his lap and screamed.

'I think she's been kidnapped. The sweet-shop woman saw her taken away in a big black car. Call the police!'

Henry brushed off the cascade of honey-bears and bananas and stood up to take his wife in a close embrace. She was weeping bitterly.

'Call the police,' she whispered into his chest. 'Call the police.'

He shook her gently. 'Hang on, dear girl, let's not go off half-cocked. If she's been kidnapped for money then we must wait for a ransom note. If we bring the police into it they might hurt her ... they might...' He could not go on.

Jack Leonard handed him a whisky and soda which was mostly whisky.

They settled down to wait. Henry Maldon would have preferred flying over Antarctica in a blizzard.

CHAPTER FOUR

All Art is quite useless
Picture of Dorian Gray, Oscar Wilde

'Miss Amelia McNaughton, Miss Fisher,' announced Mr Butler.

Phryne and the young doctor had been getting on famously when a faltering ring of the doorbell had interrupted their flirtation. Phryne pulled her mind back to the task at hand and took a good look at the daughter of the McNaughton house. It was not encouraging. Amelia was tall and thin, with ruthlessly cropped, mousy hair and blotchy skin. She had beautifully shaped hands, long and white, but they were stained with paint and the nails had been gnawed down to the quick. She had obviously dressed in a hurry or in the dark, for she was wearing a shapeless knitted skirt, darned black lisle stockings, and an overlarge shirt and jacket. Her pale blue eyes flicked from Phryne to Dr Fielding and she was biting her lower lip.

Dr Fielding stood up and offered her his chair.

'Please sit down, Miss McNaughton, and have some tea,' invited Phryne. 'Your mother is quite all right for the moment. Dr Fielding has given her a sedative. You must be cold. Mr B., could you get more tea? No, on second thoughts, a cocktail would be more suitable,' she went on, observing the blue lips and the features pinched, as if with cold.

Miss McNaughton sank down into the chair and held out her gnawed fingers to the bright fire.

'Thank you, Miss Fisher. I don't know what to do. Father is dead, and Bill arrested, and mother in a state, and I've no one to turn to...'

'Have you no relatives in Melbourne who might help?'

'God, no. There's my father's brothers; Uncle Ted and Uncle Bob. Both of them worse than useless. We have never been a close family. Uncle Ted telephoned but all he wanted to say was that Father had left him some shares in his will and that now was the time to transfer them, because the market was turning down and they should be sold.'

'Charming,' commented Phryne. Dr Fielding got to his feet and kicked the fire-irons over.

'Lord, man, can't you keep your seat?' snapped Phryne. 'We have enough to worry about without you doing three rounds with the furniture. I want you here to take Mrs McNaughton home and I'd be obliged if you would stay put.'

Dr Fielding stiffened.

'I would not be remiss in my duty to the patient, but I did not wish to be third-party to a conference,' he announced. 'I shall sit in the kitchen until you are ready, Miss Fisher.'

He stalked out to be comforted by Mrs Butler with teacake.

'"It is offended: see, it stalks away,"' quoted Phryne and chuckled. 'What a strong sense of propriety, to be sure. Miss McNaughton, I am reluctant to leave you in that house with no one to look after you.'

'Oh, that's all right,' muttered Miss Mc-Naughton gracelessly. 'Mama's maid was my nurse. We shall do well together. And now that Father is ... is dead, Mama's nerves will be better.'

'If your father was anything like your brother Bill, then he must have been rather ... er ... robust in his private life.'

'He was a loud, crass, overbearing selfish

brute,' said Miss McNaughton flatly. 'He nearly drove Mother mad and he always treated me like a chattel.' She gulped her cocktail thirstily. 'Do you know what he wanted to do, Miss Fisher? In this year of 1928? He wanted to marry me off.'

'How medieval,' said Phryne. 'How did you feel about that? I should have dug in my heels.'

'So I did,' agreed the young woman rather muzzily. Mr Butler's cocktails had some authority. 'I told him I'd see him damned first. I have my own man.'

She cast Phryne a glance both proud and oddly ashamed.

'Oh, good. An artist, is he?'

Miss McNaughton's pale eyes glowed.

'He's a sculptor. He is in the forefront of modern art. Father would not have spat on him, because he is a foreigner.'

'I have always been interested in art,' agreed Phryne. 'What sort of foreigner?'

'An Italian. Paolo Raguzzi. You will have heard of him, if you are interested in art.'

'I haven't investigated the Melbourne art world at all, Miss McNaughton, I have only been here for three months. However, are you now intending to marry?'

'Of course.'

'You must invite me to the wedding. Now, perhaps we had better get your mother home. I'll come too, and have a squiz at the scene of the crime. What is the name of the investigating policeman?'

'I can't remember... Barton, was it? No, Benton. Detective-inspector Benton.'

'Right. How did you get here? Do you have a car?'

'Yes, I took Father's Bentley. He didn't know that I could drive. We'd better call back that doctor.'

Phryne rang the electric bell. When Mr Butler appeared, she asked for Dr Fielding. He came, in offended silence, certified Mrs McNaughton safe to drive, and carried her out to the car. Phryne saw that although he was tall and clumsy, he carried the not inconsiderable burden of the unconscious woman without apparent effort.

Phryne took hat, gloves and coat from Dot and dismissed her at the door.

'You stay here and mind the phone, Dot. Call me at the McNaughton's if anything interesting happens. Stay home, I might need you. Do you have Bert's number?'

'Yes, Miss. Be careful, Miss.'

'I'm not going flying again today, Dot, I promise. Have a nice cosy evening, and tell

Mrs B. that I shall be dining out.' Phryne sailed down the steps in a red cloth coat with an astrakhan collar which made her look as though she was wearing a sheep around her neck. Her hat was black felt and her boots Russian leather. Dr Fielding straightened up from depositing Mrs Mc-Naughton in the car and came face-to-face with her. She smelt bewitchingly of 'Jicky'.

'Do not be offended, Doctor. One is prone to be sharp when one is upset. I beg your pardon, and I hope to see you again in a less clinical circumstance. Come to dinner on Thursday at seven.'

She gave him a dazzling smile and her strong, scented hand. He floated off down the street to his Austin in a strange state between insult and adoration. Phryne smiled after him, satisfied with the impression she had created, and hopped into the Bentley next to the sleeping woman.

Miss McNaughton was a good, if reckless driver, and Phryne had nothing to do during the drive but to cushion Mrs McNaughton against the bumps. Amelia McNaughton took corners as though they were a personal affront.

After about half-an-hour, during which Phryne sustained a number of bruises, the car turned and swept up the paved drive of a big, modern house. Miss Amelia leapt out of the car and ran into the house to find aid in carrying her mother. Phryne eased herself out of her position between Mrs Mc-Naughton and the door and got out.

It was three o'clock on a fine, breezy, winter's day. The beech and elm trees that lined the drive had lost all of their foliage, but the house evidently kept a gardener, for there was not a leaf to be seen lying on the smooth lawns. The house was of a modern shape; cubist, with a mural consisting of slabs of rainbow colours over the front door. The mural was reminiscent of art deco jewellery, and Phryne like it, especially against the smooth, flat planes of the building. Without the decoration the house would have been just a collection of different sized boxes in a cool grey brick.

The designer of this residence had decided that privacy was the keynote; and had placed the house in the very centre of the available space and surrounded it with a formal garden on one side, a kitchen garden at the back, and rolling park-like garden with tennis-court on the sides facing the road. No other houses could be seen. The house appeared as a little island of habitation in a wild and possibly dangerous wood. Even the traffic could not be heard, and at the bottom of the garden was the Studley Park rift. This was a deep valley with the river at the bottom and untouched forest occupying the slopes. It would be a very lonely place for the nervous. Phryne wondered how Mrs McNaughton liked living there and whether she had been consulted at all in the building of it.

Amelia returned with a gardener and a stout woman in an apron. Together they lifted Mrs McNaughton and bore her into the hall and up the stairs to a small room with a narrow bed.

'Surely this isn't her room?' asked Phryne in surprise.

'Yes, since she stopped sleeping with Father. He wouldn't let her have another room. He said that she could stay with him in the big room or have this, so she chose this. She says it makes her feel safe; there are no windows, just the light from the stairwell. But she doesn't have to lock herself in any more,' said Miss McNaughton as she straightened her mother's limbs and composed them for further slumber. 'And here's one door he won't batter against again.'

She stepped out of the room, leaving the

stout woman to sit by the bed, and pointed to dents and cracks in the wood. The door had done nobly in fending off the master of the house. The timbers had cracked a little, but they had not broken.

'Ah,' said Phryne, deeply disgusted and wondering whether she wanted to find out who killed Mr McNaughton.

'He used to hit her – and me, too,' said Miss McNaughton matter-of-factly. 'But he stopped hitting me because I said I'd leave and that I'd take Mother with me. That frightened him, he was terrified of scandal, and I could have made a very impressive one. He didn't beat Mother while I was here, but I wasn't here very often. I am at the Gallery School, you know.'

'Yes, your brother told me you were an artist. And Bunji still has your watercolour of a plane on her wall.' Phryne was fishing. In all this time Miss McNaughton had not mentioned her brother.

'Bill didn't think that I could paint. He has the artistic sensibilities of an ox. And he called Paolo a greasy little dago. But he didn't kill my father,' stated Miss McNaughton, stopping on the stairs with one hand on the bannister. 'If Bill had killed Father he would have announced it to the world. He

83

would not have run away. He takes after Father – everything he does has to be right. He and Father never made a mistake or offered an apology in their lives. Bill would have stood over the body and announced that he had a perfect right to kill his own father if he liked, and would anyone care to argue about it? I don't know who killed Father, but it was not Bill. I don't care if you don't find who killed him. In fact I'd rather you did not. Father had thousands of people who rightly hated him and any one of them is more valuable than Father. I loathed him and I hated what he did to me and my mother; do you know, after he had pounded on Mother's door and been refused, he used to come and make an attempt on me?'

'Did he succeed?' asked Phryne gently. Miss McNaughton stared through Phryne with her pale blue eyes.

'When I was younger,' she said quietly. 'He managed to catch me in the bathroom. Twice. After that I put a chair under the handle. He used to stand outside and bellow at me to let him in. I considered it, because it might have calmed him down, but I couldn't, I really couldn't. That's why Paolo is the only man I have ever loved – could ever love. He took such pains with me, he was so patient when I flinched and cried, and ... and...'

'I know,' observed Phryne quietly. 'But it happens to a lot of women. You and I are fortunate in that we have found lovers who could coax us out of our shells. Come down, Miss McNaughton, and let's get warm. Then you can show me your work.'

'Please call me Amelia,' said Miss Mc-Naughton suddenly. 'You are the only person apart from Paolo that I have told ... come and sit by the fire in the drawing room, and I'll bring the stuff down. You might not like it,' she warned, and ran upstairs again.

Phryne was shown into a fine big drawing room with Chinese furnishings. The ceiling was lacquered red and the walls were hung with scroll painting and embroideries. Several brocade garments decorated the chimney piece, and the chairs were pierced and decorated blackwood, with silk cushions and legs carved with lions and clouds.

On the mantleshelf stood one free-standing jade sculpture of a rather self-satisfied dragon devouring a deer. The deer's eyes reminded Phryne uncomfortably of Mrs McNaughton's and Phryne turned away from it to study the silk painting by the square, latticed window. She recognized it as a copy of a famous artist. It was 'Two Gentlemen Discoursing Upon Fish'. 'Look how the fish disport themselves in the clear water,' enthused one gentleman. 'That is how the Almighty gives pleasure to fish'. 'You are not a fish,' objected the other. 'How do you know what gives pleasure to fish?' 'You are not I,' replied the first. 'How do you know that I do not know what gives pleasure to fish?' And that, of course, was unanswerable.

What did any of us know about the other, mused Phryne. If she had met the late and entirely unlamented Mr McNaughton, would she have known that he was a domestic tyrant, who when refused by his wife had sexually assaulted his daughter?

Amelia came in with a rush, and shoved a portfolio of impressive proportions into Phryne's arms.

'I'll see about the tea,' she muttered, and rushed out again. Phryne diagnosed artistic modesty. She emptied the folio onto the blackwood table and spread out the contents. There were watercolours, a few oil sketches, and charcoal and red chalk drawings. They were good, Phryne found with pleasure. It was always easier to genuinely praise than to try and find something nice to say about rubbish.

There were three watercolours of aeroplanes, with a pale wash of sky behind them. There were sharp, clear pencil drawings of flowers and birds, exhibiting signs of a Chinese phase. There were several rather muddy landscapes and a clever cubist house; but Miss McNaughton's real skill was in portraiture. With chalk or charcoal she could catch a likeness more clearly than a photograph. Here was Bill in flying togs, hulking and self-confident, but with a hint of reckless good-humour which Phryne had also seen. Here was her mother, in pastels, worn and lined, with the fluffy, harried look so familiar to Phryne. It was evident that Amelia's skills were not yet perfect, she was prone to a certain lack of confidence in her lines and some of her colours might have been bolder. Phryne searched through the portraits with delight. Here was a group of children, somewhat after Murillo but none-the-less charming. Here were eleven studies of a cat; she had caught the creature's elusive muscularity under the fur. Here was a swarthy man, thin and intense, with deep eyes and charming faun-like face; he had pointed ears, and the whole gave an impression of power and patience. Phryne was reminded of a Medici, and wondered if it was a copy of a Renaissance work. She turned the oil over. 'Paolo'. Aha. Good looking, but not beautiful. Deep, and a strong personality. Such a man must have made a potent impression on Amelia, who was not familiar with any powerful man who did not brawl and rape. She looked forward to meeting him.

There was a portrait of a woman. Phryne recognized her friend Isola di Fraoli, the ballad singer. She had caught her perfectly; the mass of black hair, the glint of earrings, the deep bosom and rounded arms and the wicked, penetrating half-smile. The last oil was a portrait of a man. Broad and tall but running to fat, he stood with legs straddled, dominating the artist with his presence. He had a jowled, big-boned face, mottled with red across the cheeks and nose. One hand was clenched and the mouth was open, as if in command. It was just a shade this side of caricature, and so carefully deliniated that it was obvious that the artist hated every line in him. Being an artist, however, she had dealt honestly with him. Phryne did not need to turn it over. The resemblance to Bill was marked. This was Amelia's father. Phryne regretted that she might have to discover who murdered him. He was the essence of everything she did not like about the male sex.

Amelia and the tea entered simultaneously. Phryne took a cup and commented 'You have a great deal of skill, Amelia. Would you sell me some of these? I've just moved into a new house and I'm decorating.'

'I can't sell them – they are only sketches. Take what you want, Miss Fisher. I would like to have some of my work in your house.'

'Call me Phryne, and I insist on paying. I wouldn't have someone say that I exploited you, especially since I shall make a packet on them when you are famous.'

'Take whichever you like,' blushed Amelia. 'Five pounds each – that's what students usually charge. Do you really like them?'

'Yes,' said Phryne sorting rapidly. 'Your professors must have told you that you have an uncommon gift for portraiture. These sketches of the cat are good, too. Have you seen that page of drawings by Leonardo of the cats, turning into dragons? Very hard to draw, cats. There's a bony shape under the skin and you have caught the furriness very well. I'll have the cats, they can go along the stairs, and these chalks, one of the Gipsy Moth, I learned to fly in one of them –

lovely little 'bus. Also the children, though they are derivative, don't you think? Do you like children?'

'I love children. I want lots of them. Now Father is ... now Father is dead, I shall have my own money and Paolo and I can get married. We shall have a house in Canton near the galleries with a studio for him and a studio for me and lots of nurseries.'

'Why haven't you married before?' asked Phryne, adding Paolo, Bill, and Isola to her pile. Amelia wriggled with embarassment.

'Paolo wanted to. He's quite well-off, he's the son of an industrialist. His father disowned him but he has an income from his mother. But I wasn't sure, and I wanted to...'

'To be sure. How long have you known him?'

'Two years. I am sure, now. It is just that Father said such awful things about him, and even hired a private detective to follow him around and to see if he was sleeping with his models.'

'And was he?'

'Oh, yes, but that doesn't matter to me. I know that he loves me. He has put such a lot of work into me that he values me. One always prizes the object on which one has lavished the greatest amount of effort. Take that portrait of Father. I hated him. But to paint him, I had to look at him quite otherwise than usual: I had to examine him as an object, not as a loathsome man who tormented me. I stopped being afraid of him after that. Somehow the process of painting him had disinfected him.'

'I know exactly what you mean,' said Phryne. 'May I have the portrait? Perhaps you would like to keep it. Apart from the Paolo, I think it is your best work.'

'Take it. I was going to burn it.'

'That would be a pity,' said Phryne. She bound up the rejects in the portfolio and wrote out a cheque.

'Perhaps you would consider a commission,' she added. 'I have a full length female nude – you may have seen it...'

'Yes. 'La Source'. It's you, isn't it. A bit Pre-Raphaelite, but skilful. Do you want something to match?'

'Yes, a male nude in the same pose. Do you draw from the figure? Or haven't you got up to that yet?'

'Yes, but it's difficult. In oil? And the same size? Let me have the dimensions, and I'll see what I can do. I haven't done a big oil. Father would never give me the money for enough paint, and students aren't supposed to sell their work. There's an acrobat who does some modelling – lovely body, all muscle, but light. My friend Sally did an Eros of him which was super. I'll try it, now I can afford the materials.'

'Good. Now, give me another cup of tea and let's get down to business. Have you a family lawyer? We ought to get Bill out of the cooler if we can.'

'Get him out? But he's been arrested.'

'Yes, but we might be able to bail him.'

'Oh. No, we haven't a lawyer who does criminal matters.'

'Leave it to me, I know just the person. Where does Paolo live? I'd like to see his work.'

Amelia wrote down the address. She was uneasy. She was about to speak when a scruffy maid ran in and announced shrilly: 'That cop's here again, Miss.'

'Put your cap straight,' ordered Phryne. 'Wipe your face on that apron and stand up. A tragedy in the family is no excuse for panic. There. Now, be a good girl. We all need your help, you know. Where would the house be without you?' Phryne smiled into wide brown eyes and tucked a whisp of hair back under the cap.

'There. Now, who is at the door?'

'Detective-inspector Benton, Miss Amelia,' announced the maid and walked proudly out.

'Phryne,' cried Amelia, 'you are wonderful. Please don't leave me.'

'I shall be here. Sit down again.'

Amelia obeyed. The maid returned and announced sedately 'Detective-inspector Benton, Miss Amelia.'

She cast Phryne a dignified glance and escorted a tubby man into the room. He was red-faced and almost comic, but his dark-brown eyes were sharp and shrewd.

At half-past three Molly Maldon and her husband walked to the lolly shop to cross-examine the shopkeeper's son Jimmy. The child was an unpleasant, sharp stripling, with a spotty face and oily fingernails. Molly, however, was prepared to love anyone who might lead her to Candida, and she asked as gently as any woman seducing an uncertain lover.

'Did you notice a big black car here at lunch-time, Jimmy?'

'Yeah,' drawled the youth. 'Bentley, 1926, black, in a terrible state of polish.'

'Did you see a little girl get into the car?'

asked Henry. Jimmy smothered a yawn and Molly bit her lip. Boxing the little thug's ears would probably prove counter-productive.

'Yes, I saw her, they kind of dragged her into the back seat. Leather upholstery,' he added unhelpfully. 'Red leather.'

'Did you notice the number?'

'Some of it. There was mud on the number plate. I reckon it was KG 12 something. Couldn't read the last digit. Sorry. Mum, when's dinner? I'm starving.'

Henry Maldon took Molly's arm before she could do something hasty and dropped a shilling into the boy's ready palm.

'Thanks, son,' he said heavily. Jimmy yawned again.

CHAPTER FIVE

She speaks poniards and every word stabs
Much Ado About Nothing, Shakespeare

'How do you do. My name is Phryne Fisher. I undertake investigations and I have been retained by the McNaughton family to act for them in this matter.'

The policeman took up a commanding position at the mantlepiece and glanced quizzically at Phryne.

'There is no room for amateurs in murder, Miss Fisher,' said the policeman condescendingly. 'But I am sure that you will be a comfort to the ladies.'

'I hope that I shall,' replied Phryne with all the sweetness of a chocolate-coated razor-blade. 'And I hope that you will allow a mere amateur to observe your methods. I am certain that I will learn a lot from your procedures. After all, it is seldom that I have the chance of getting so close to a famous detective like yourself.' Amelia looked up. Surely the man was not going to be taken in by this load of old cobblers? It seemed that Phryne had not under-estimated the recept-iveness of the detective to a bit of the old oil. He softened and became positively polite.

'Of course, I shall be delighted to instruct you, Miss Fisher,' he purred. 'But I came to tell Miss Amelia that she should get a lawyer for her brother. He's coming up before the Magistrates tomorrow morning, and he should be represented.'

'Thank you, I shall do that,' said Amelia. 'Are you certain that my brother killed my father, Detective-inspector?'

'Well, Miss, he hasn't admitted it. He says that he came home last night and intended to have a discussion with Mr McNaughton. He admits that he had continual arguments with his father, and that they became violent at times.'

'Yes, that is true,' sighed Amelia.

'He wanted to drive his father to a meeting at the aerodrome so that the mother would not be upset by their argument,' said the detective-inspector. 'He says you suggested it, Miss Fisher. He waited for his father until four o'clock then gave up on him and went for a walk in the park. He says he met no one except an old man with a sack over his shoulder and a young woman, who ran past in a bathing suit.'

'So have you found the girl or the old man?' asked Phryne respectfully. 'I'm sure that you are looking for them.'

'Well, yes,' the policeman paused. 'Yes, so to speak, but we haven't found them. And we won't. I don't for a moment believe that there was a man or a girl, or that he went for a walk in the valley. I am sure that he killed your father, Miss McNaughton.'

'Why?' asked Phryne artlessly.

'Why? Well, such things are not nice for a young woman, Miss Fisher.'

'Ah. Suppose you take me out to look at where it happened. I have always wanted to see the scene of the crime.' Phryne wondered if she was laying it on too thick but it seemed that for this obtuse man no flattery could be too gross.

'Very well, Miss,' agreed the Detective-inspector. 'Come along with me.'

'You stay here, Amelia,' instructed Phryne. 'Have some more tea. I shall be quite safe with Detective-inspector Benton.'

Amelia, open mouthed, smothered a giggle in her teacup.

Benton led Phryne out of the house and along a fine mossy path to the tennis-court. It was beautifully kept, with a grass surface as smooth as a bowling green. The lines were freshly painted and the net was not in evidence.

'This grass will not hold footprints,' commented Benton. 'But here are the holes caused by Mrs McNaughton's high-heels. She ran off the path here, you see, stood for a moment where the heels have sunk in deep, then ran back to the house. The dog's footprints aren't heavy enough to make a mark except on the flowerbeds. The body lay here.'

Phryne could see that it had. There was a sanded puddle of blood and grey matter, indicating that a very heavy blow had killed Mr McNaughton.

Benton hovered at Phryne's elbow, ready to catch her if she should faint. She did not, however, even pale.

'A head wound,' she said. 'How bad? How heavy a blow?'

'A very heavy blow, Miss. He was hit with a stone, a big rock.'

'Were there any fingerprints on the rock?'

'No, Miss, the surface was too rough to take prints.'

'How do you know it was the murder weapon?'

'Blood and brains all over it,' said the

policeman, aiming to shock this young woman out of her unnatural composure.

'And why should Bill McNaughton have delivered it?'

'It was a good, solid skull-cracking blow, Miss. Split the head almost in two. No woman could have delivered it.'

'I see.' Phryne scanned the garden. There was not a gap in the flowerbeds, which were in any case edged with wood.

'Where did the rock come from?' she asked. Benton spluttered.

'Where did the...'

'Yes, where did it come from? Look around. There's not a stone in sight. In the opportunistic crime which you describe, the murderer would have snatched up anything to hit his father with and left him lying. You are assuming that Mr McNaughton followed his father out here to continue the argument and it developed into a fight? And that under the influence of fury, Bill McNaughton went beserk and just donged his father with whatever was to hand? Is that not the idea?'

'Yes. I take your point, Miss. This must have been premeditated. He must have had the rock all ready, then lured his father out here and killed him.'

Phryne briefly wondered how anyone could cling to a theory with this intransigence, in the face of all the evidence.

Phryne had moved away to lean against the old oak which had one branch overhanging the lawn. She patted it idly – she loved trees – and looked up into the branches.

'There's a scar on that branch,' she observed. 'Something hung here.'

'Quite the little detective, aren't you, Miss? That was a swing – a tyre. Miss McNaughton put it there for the neighbouring children. Very fond of children, Miss McNaughton,' said the detective-inspector, evidently approving of this womanly passion. 'The cook tells me she was always inviting them in for tea on Sundays, and playing games with them. We took the tyre away to be tested but there are no bloodstains on it. Miss McNaughton will be able to put the swing back, if she wants to. After the place has been cleaned up, of course. Nice young woman, pity she is so plain. Should have children of her own.'

Phryne agreed. Miss McNaughton would enjoy having children of her own. She withdrew her gaze from the tree.

'So Mrs McNaughton came out here – why was Mr McNaughton here?'

'He must have come out here to continue his argument with his son, of course. Then it developed into a fight, no, hang on, there's the point about the stone. Bill McNaughton brought his father out here, and had the rock ready, and asked his father to look at something, perhaps, and then bang, then he panics, leaves the stone, and runs off down the valley to recover himself.'

'Would he have had blood on him?'

'I asked the police surgeon that, Miss. He says that if he hit him from behind, which is what he thinks happened, then he wouldn't have to have any blood on him. I thought like you, Miss,' continued Benton, honouring Phryne by implying that they shared the same reasoning, 'I thought that he was going down to the river to wash. But he still had the same clothes on when we apprehended him last night, and there ain't no mark on them.'

'I see. Well, watching your methods has been most illuminating, Detective-inspector. Thank you so much.' Phryne took her leave and went back to the house. Danny the dog cried after her from where he was tied in the kitchen garden.

'Amelia, I have to go and find a lawyer for Bill,' she called into the Chinese room. 'Give me my paintings and see what you can do about getting me a taxi.'

'I'll drive you,' offered Amelia. Phryne shook her head.

'I need you here, and so does your mother.'

The maid went off to telephone for a cab, and Amelia seized Phryne by the sleeve.

'Do you think Bill did it?' she breathed.

'I don't know. Tell me, the children who play in the garden, did your father know about them?'

'Not until recently – he was always out during Sunday. He came home early last week and caught me with them, and threw them out, the brute. The poor little things haven't anywhere else to play, and their mothers know that they are safe with me. I used to give them tea. And cakes. Bill likes children, too. He rigged up that swing with the tyre for them.' Amelia shuddered suddenly, and all the colour drained out of her face.

'The police took the tyre away, but they said I can have it back. I'll have to find somewhere else to put it.'

'Have you seen the children since your father died?'

'No, they have stayed away, poor things, I suppose that they are frightened.'

'Why don't you invite them again?' suggested Phryne. 'They will make you feel better, and you can have them in the house, now.'

'What a good idea. I can have a party! Oh, but not with Bill–'

'Nonsense. Have your party. Let me know when it is. I like children, too,' lied Phryne. 'Your brother will come up at the Melbourne Magistrates' Court tomorrow at ten. Perhaps you should be there, and bring some money.'

'Where shall I get money?'

'Oh, dear, have you not got your father's bankbooks? Did he have a safe in the house?'

'Of course. The detective-inspector brought the keys back. The police have already searched it. Come on, let's have a look.'

She led the way up stairs to a huge bedroom, decorated in the extreme of modernity. The walls were jazz-coloured and the stark gigantic bed looked like it was made of industrial piping.

'Did your father really like all this stuff?' asked Phryne, as Amelia swung a picture aside and unlocked the safe.

'Father? I don't know,' admitted Amelia, her brow furrowing as she spun the combination wheel. 'He had the house built in the most modern style and then said that the inside had to match the outside. The designer did all the rest. It was very expensive. Ah. There's the click. I remembered the combination correctly after all.' The safe door swung open and Phryne received an armload of paper, jewel cases and a document case.

'There are mother's sapphires – he told her he had sold them,' observed Amelia, opening the blue-velvet boxes. 'And Granny's pearls, and Great-Granny's emerald set. Oh, and here is the enamel from that German exhibition.'

Amelia put into Phryne's hand one of the most beautiful pieces of jewellery she had ever seen. It was a mermaid in enamel, seated on a baroque pearl. Her delicately modelled body was of ivory; her hair was malachite, and tiny emeralds sparkled as her eyes. Bronze threads shone in her seaweed-green hair.

'Isn't she pretty? Even Father appreciated her. Is there any money?'

'Yes, here's two thou. in notes, that should be enough to spring Bill and pay the wages until the estate is settled. Hang on while I just have a bit of a look through these papers.'

The document case contained several reports from the 'Discretion Private Investigations Agency' which listed Mrs McNaughton's movements through a whole week. They concluded that there was nothing suspicious in her actions. Did Mr McNaughton know about Gerald? Phryne wondered. Amelia pinned the mermaid brooch to the bosom of her drab dress and contemplated herself artlessly in the mirror which covered one whole wall of the room. It was all lights and surfaces and Phryne felt it to be intensely uncomfortable. The agency reported that Paolo Raguzzi was known to be sleeping with two of his models, and included names and dates. As a strategy designed to detach Amelia, it had not been any more successful than it deserved. Phryne leafed through several bank statements and cheque books and a pile of share certificates. The deeds to the house were there, as was the will.

She glanced through it. The bulk of the estate went to the wife, as long as she should not remarry. Ten thousand pounds was left to 'my daughter, Amelia, as long as she shall not marry'. The old bastard, thought Phryne, trying to hang on to his control of his family even after he was dead.

A firm of solicitors were the executors. The estate seemed to be worth about fifty thousand. This did not include the house which was freehold. Phryne reflected that Mrs McNaughton could live very comfortably on the interest.

'Here's the will, do you know what's in it?'

'Oh, yes. He's left me some money provided I don't marry. But he can't stop me from having Granny's money. It was left to me but he took it and invested it and wouldn't give me an allowance. The papers should be there ... yes.' She plucked an old parchment and probate out of the pile. "To my grandaughter Amelia the sum of five thousand pounds". That will keep me for life. I don't want any of my father's money.'

Fine words, thought Phryne. I wonder if Paolo thinks the same.

'Did you tell Paolo about the will?'

'Oh, yes,' said Amelia indifferently. 'He just said that he would expect such a thing from Father. Well, if that is all, Phryne, your taxi should be waiting, and I'll put all this stuff back in the safe. I will see you tomorrow?'

'Yes, I shall be there. Take heart, my dear. I shall get your brother out of prison.'

'Thanks,' murmured Amelia. Phryne took her leave and ordered the taxi to take her to Carlton.

At the door of a rather dingy office building

she asked her cab to wait and leapt up the stairs, taking the route indicated by the brass plate 'Henderson, Jones, and Mayhew'. Luckily, the light was still on, although the secretary had gone home.

'Hello, Jilly, old bean, are you home?'

'Certainly, come through, Phryne. What brings you to this haunt of probate and miscellaneous offences?'

Jillian Henderson was a short, stout woman of about forty, who had taken her father's place in his firm. She was still a junior partner and prone to collect more than her share of divorces and family problems. None the less she had built up a flourishing little practice in crime and was always on the lookout for a murder, where she thought she would make her reputation.

'Got a murder for you, Jilly, and you'll have to apply for bail for him tomorrow morning, can you manage?'

'Oh, Phryne, how super! A murder of my very own. What's his name?'

'Bill McNaughton. You might have read about it in the newspaper. Have you no fire in these rooms? I'm perishing.'

Phryne went into Jillian's office, and ensconced herself in front of a meagre kerosene heater.

'Tell me all about it.'

Phryne recounted the history and proceedings of the investigation, and Jillian pursed her lips.

'And you are going to find the real murderer for him, are you?'

'I'm going to try.'

'Well, think carefully before you tell me what you find. They have a very slim case against your Bill. His fingerprints are not on the stone, and he says he was in the river valley. Two people are supposed to have seen him.'

'Yes. And he is definitely not my Bill.'

'Now what if you find these two people and they can't remember seeing Bill? People are very unobservant. I would not trust any eyewitness evidence if it was served up to me on a plate. It is most unreliable. If you don't find them, I can suggest that they exist but just haven't been found. If you find 'em and they can be discounted as evidence, the prosecution has a weapon. See?'

'I'm shocked,' declared Phryne. 'Have you no regard for truth?'

'If you had entered the law, you will know that truth is a very dicey quality. "What is truth?" said Pilate, and I have always thought he must have been a solicitor. However, I'll apply for bail tomorrow, and see if the police have any objections. It depends on who the prosecutor is, and the informant.'

'I think the informant must be Detective-inspector Benton.' Jillian groaned, and made a note.

'I ought to charge double for dealing with him. He has a theory, I gather?'

'Yes, that Bill lured his father out onto the tennis-court and hit him with a rock imported for the purpose.'

'Then he'll stick to it through thick, thin, and soupy. I've had some struggles with him. I've never met such a stubborn man in my entire life,' said Jillian, rubbing her hands, and seeming to relish a new conflict. 'Well, well, good old Benton. This may be fun. Am I definitely retained? You have the family's authority?'

'Yes, I do, and you are retained like billy-o. Go to it and the Lord speed your foot-steps. Now I've got to go and see a sculptor. Miss McNaughton has two thou, in cash – will that cover the surety?'

'I think so. We may have to go to the Supreme Court tomorrow, if the Magistrate won't cooperate. Will the old bank account stand that?

'It will. Got to go, Jilly. See you tomorrow

at ten.'

'I shall be there,' said Jillian smugly. 'And you shall have Bill shortly after.'

Phryne retrieved her taxi and set off for the studio of Paolo Ragazzi.

CHAPTER SIX

I can resist anything except temptation
Lady Windermere's Fan, Oscar Wilde

The studio of Paolo Raguzzi was on the third floor of a rundown boarding house at the depressed end of Princes Street. Phryne trod slowly up the stairs, the lift being out of order, and knocked on a flimsy wooden door. Something loud and vaguely operatic was playing on a gramophone inside. Phryne knocked again.

The door was flung open by a girl in a coat and hat.

'Oh, good, dearie, you're just in time. He's doing his block in there. I told him that I'd have to leave early but he just keeps going on about his nymph. Good luck, and don't take no notice. He ain't bad; just loud.' So saying, she tripped lightly down the stairs and Phryne was confronted with a burst of what she assumed were swear words in Italian. They proceeded from behind a beaded curtain, and a voice yelled, 'Avanti!

Vieni, vieni qua, signorina. I haven't got all night and you're letting the cold in. Come along! I won't bite, whatever Mary told you at the door.'

This sounded promising and the voice was light and pleasant, so Phryne brushed the beads aside and went in.

The studio was a large, light room, with the winter sun fading through the skylight. At one end was the artist's living quarters, which were in neat array; at the other a bed, and a model's throne covered by a worn velvet cloth in Phryne's favourite shade of green. There was a delightful scent of buttered toast. The artist, attired in a very old shirt and flannel bags, was crunching the last crumb. He was not much taller than Phryne and had fine brown eyes, which smiled. Otherwise he looked just like his portrait.

'I'm...' began Phryne, and the artist waved his teacup.

'I'm delighted to meet you, *signorina*. You have just the limbs that I require. You can put your clothes over there, and call me when you are ready.'

This was interesting. She had been mistaken for a model. Paolo had already retreated behind the screen and Phryne had often modelled for artists in her days in the apache quarter of Paris. She shrugged out of her coat and boots and hung the rest of her clothes on the hook which seemed to have been placed there on purpose. She took her seat on the model's throne and called, 'Ready.'

Paolo, having finished his tea, appeared and flicked the cloth off a small clay model. It was a nymph, hair in disarray, accepting the embraces of a satyr with evident pleasure. The delicate limbs wrapped the hairy goat-skin haunches, and she leaned back in delight against the embracing arms. Although the detail of the genitalia was decorously covered by thigh and hand, it was evident that both bodies had just joined. The satyr was crouched, and the whole structure depended upon his cloven feet and the long legs of the nymph, whose toes were just touching the ground.

Technically, it was a difficult piece, presenting intriguing problems of mass and balance. Of itself, it glowed with an innocent eroticism and good humour.

'It is lovely,' commented Phryne. The sculptor looked as surprised as if his anatomy textbook had just spoken.

'Thank you, but the curve of this arm is not right. Will you lean back a little more, *signorina,* and bend your wrist down ... no, it does not work. You need something to embrace.' Paolo left the clay and dived for Phryne, arranging her limbs around him.

'You see, she is joined to him, thus ... move that leg a little ... and his arms are holding her weight ... thus.'

Phryne's mouth was near the artist's, and his arms were very strong. She relaxed a little, and he shook her.

'*No, no, no!* She is not languid, she is afire with passion. The body is thrust against him, with force, to engulf him. So.' He leaned forward without warning and kissed one breast, then the other. Her nipples hardened. The Renaissance head bent to suckle. Phryne gasped. Her hands tightened on his back. She arched. For a moment, he held her strongly, and he felt her tremble.

'Later. Do not move,' he said, stuffing a big cushion into her arms.

Stunned, Phryne clutched the pillow, frozen with tension into the position she had been placed. Clay flew. She heard it fall with sad little sounds to the floor. She could not see the progress of the figure, but Paolo was pleased.

'Oh, excellent, excellent ... now the shoulder ... do not move.' Phryne was torn between rage and laughter. The studio was getting very cold. She fell into her model's dreaming trance and recalled the Paris studios where her dearest friends had been surrealists. She had once been offered a Dada dinner, which consisted of boiled string. She heard the sculptor calling her as if from a long way away.

'*Vieni, carissima*. See what you have done. It is finished.'

She untangled herself from the cushion and bent her stiff limbs. Paolo seized her and rubbed her into mobility with his large, strong hands, then led her to the covered model.

'See, *bella*, what you have wrought. For weeks I have been trying to capture that curve, that intense clutch – and there it is. It is complete.'

'What shall you cast it in?'

'Silver-gilt, nothing else. Nothing else is good enough for such a work. I thank you from the bottom of my heart.'

He kissed Phryne enthusiastically and she discovered that her aroused passion had been frozen, not absent. It was now thawing.

She beat the sculptor to the warm blankets of his bed by a short half-head, and wrapped them both. The blankets were clean, as was the sculptor. He smelt delightfully of clay and leather and tobacco and something vaguely herbal. She continued to kiss him, caressing the pointed ears, the mobile mouth and the long, beautiful line of muscle from back to buttock. He laid his head upon her breast and sighed with pleasure.

'Ah, *bella* how fortunate I am to find you. Sure a pure line; so delicate, so true.' He rubbed his face across her breasts, catching at the nipples as his mouth passed. 'And now, do you want me?'

Phryne, who had always been a woman of strong passions, was decided.

'I do,' she answered, then clutched him close.

Paolo was a good lover; deft, sensitive and passionate. What woman could ask more? As he lay with her he breathed praises into her ear; *bella, bella, bellissima.*

Satisfied, Phryne kissed her lover firmly, got up, and donned her clothes.

'You must go? But I do not even know your name,' he cried.

'You are coming too. I'm taking you to dinner. Is there anything good around here? My name is Phryne Fisher. I'm investigating McNaughton's murder.'

116

'Then you are not a professional model,' concluded the artist in triumph. 'I knew it. No model could have made me finish my nymph. Only a new young lady could be a sufficient inspiration. Have you seen my fiancé? Is she well? She told me not to come to her, or I should not be here.'

'Amelia is fine. I have just come from there. I wanted to ask you some questions about the matter. But I was diverted.'

'Ah, *signorina,* do not think that I am insensible of the honour. I, too, have been much diverted. But now I shall dress and we shall go to dinner. I thank you for your care of Amelia. As it is not possible for even the most foolish of policemen to think that I had anything to do with the murder of that swine, I shall go to Amelia tomorrow, and I shall not leave her. Especially since I have finished the nymph,' added Paolo artlessly.

'Why Amelia, above all the others?' asked Phryne suddenly. Paolo had found trousers and boots but could not locate his shirt. He searched hopelessly, then found it on the model's throne, whence he had flung it.

'Why Amelia?' repeated Phryne. 'It is not her money; she gets none under her father's will.'

'That I know. It is nothing. She has a little

money, but it is not that. I could have had Princesses – and have, in my time,' he added complacently through the folds of the shirt. 'Look at that shelf, over there, *bella*.'

Phryne surveyed the shelf. There were five nude statues, each beautifully modelled, and each was of the same woman. Paolo breathed in Phryne's ear.

'Look at her. She is perfect. The length of limb, the straight back; for a sculptor she is perfect in every way. You should see her as I do, *bella* – without her clothes. You, now, are pretty – in fact I would say that you are striking. You would never be mistaken for anyone but yourself. If you were modelled as Venus or Diana or St Joan everyone would say, "Ah! Miss Fisher," because you have the distinctive face. But the body pure of line, yes, delicate of bone, assuredly. But only that. As you age – I beg your pardon, *bella* – you will sag like every other woman. You will still be beautiful and distinctive. But my Amelia will be a sculptor's dream; old, sagging, pregnant. She is the universal woman. When I met her she was ashamed – her father was a brute, a swine, a beast. But I coaxed her, I flattered her, I taught her to pose nude and enjoy her body, and now she is complete. I could never find another like her. Money, pah! A body like that you could search a century for and never find. It is undoubtedly due to the special intervention of St Anthony, who has guarded me all my life, that I have found her and I would not risk losing her for the undoubted pleasure of wiping her detestable father off the face of the earth.'

'Ah,' agreed Phryne. 'Dinner?'

'We shall go to the Café Royale,' announced Paolo. 'If you are paying. You can ask me whatever you like, and I shall answer, *bellisima.*'

He had found all his clothes. He took his hat, keys and cigarettes and led the bemused Phryne out of the studio.

The Café Royale was the haunt of bohemians and artists. Phryne had always meant to go there. One entered through a small, iron-studded door which led into a cobwebby cellar with many barrels, and then into a large, smoky room with lanterns hanging from the beams. It was a little like the Hall of the Mountain King and a little like the hold of a ship. It smelt delightfully of garlic, roasting meat, Turkish cigarettes and coffee. The log fire had been burning all day and the smoke added to the aromatic, raffish air.

Phryne was escorted to a table with ceremony by three waiters, who took her coat and supplied her with a bottle and a glass. The wine was Lambrusco, a strong sweet red wine of the Po Valley. It was just what was needed on a frosty night.

Paolo was known in the Café Royale and the proprietor himself came out of the kitchen to welcome him and his guest.

Paolo leaned back in the wooden chair and raised his glass.

'I have completed my nymph, with the admirable assistance of this young lady. It has been a severe labour. Therefore, Guiseppe, we require food. What is good tonight?'

Guiseppe smiled a huge smile which revealed a treasury of gold teeth, and began to speak expansively in Italian.

'Will you allow me to order?' asked Paolo. Phryne nodded, impressed with his manners.

Guiseppe concluded his address with a wide gesture, and bellowed an order into the kitchen. Paolo poured Phryne another glass of wine.

'Why did you come to Australia, Paolo?'

'Ah. I come from *Firenze* – Florence. You have been there?' Phryne nodded again. The faun's countenance was fascinating in the flickering light, and she privately congratulated Amelia on her luck, or judgement.

'Then you know that it is a city filled with art. If one is in the least susceptible, then one must appreciate it. My father makes cement. I believe that it is good cement, and he has made a fortune out of it. I do not like cement, and I have no head for business. When he sent me out on errands, I was to be found gazing with awe at the great gates, or the Roman marbles, or the bronzes in the public squares. This did not please my father. He sent me to oversee the cement works. I could not command the workers, and in any case I discovered Carrara marble was also mined there. When he told me I would never see his face again until I stopped being an artist, ah, *bella*. I thought of all the faces I would create and all the beauty I would have to surrender. My father has not such a compelling countenance to enable me to renounce all the world's beauties. So he cut me out of his will. He is, in any case, a peasant, and peasants do not appreciate art. My mother was from a minor aristocratic house. She gave me all her money and said, "Go forth, my son, and create beautiful things. Come and see me when your father is dead. But you must leave Italy." I took half of the money and I was free in the world. Ah. Here is the good Guiseppe with the pasta. This you will enjoy, *bella*. It is as I ate it in the old country, but better. Here the ingredients are of the quality which one cannot afford in Italy.'

Guiseppe set down a dish of strange green noodles, mixed through with oil, olives, chicken livers, onions and mushrooms. It smelt delicious. Paolo ladled out a plateful then continued.

'I then asked myself, where should I go? America? I did not like the Americans I had met. I wandered down to the docks in Marseille, and sat down in a tavern to think. There I met some of the crew of an Australian ship. They were stokers and boilerminders, and such faces! Such bodies! I speak from an artistic point of view, you understand, I have no sexual interest in men.' He took several huge mouthfuls of the succulent pasta, and waved his fork for emphasis.

'They asked me to sit down, and I shared several bottles with them. It enabled me to try out my English on a native speaker, but I could not understand them at first. The accent is very marked, you understand. The ship was leaving that night. They took me on as the keeper of a racehorse, whose stableman had been arrested by the police for an affray in a brothel. Marseilles is a very rough place. I have always been fond of horses, so I agreed to take care of "Dark Day" until we reached Australia. He was going on to New Zealand. A stallion. The struggles I had with him! A beast of great pride; but the spirit of a demon. Later his owner paid me three hundred pounds for the bronze I made of him. I found his cure, though.'

'What was that?'

'When he would rear and scream – so that I feared for his knees and even more for my life – I fed him honey-soaked oatmeal and brandy. He did not relish the taste at first, but after a while he would sidle over and try to seize the bottle from my hand. It would make him calm and happy again and lie down in his stall. Fortunately horses do not suffer from the hangover. I got to Melbourne and left "Dark Day" with regret. He was sorry to part with me, too, but I instructed his new keeper about the brandy. He arrived safe in New Zealand and sired many children. I wandered around Melbourne until I found this place, and Guiseppe took me to his chest. He found me a studio and introduced me to many artists, and I have not had to touch my mother's money. I am a good sculptor. And I like it here. The food is good and the climate is like Florence and the women are beautiful and complaisant. A reasonable man cannot ask for more. Then, more was given to me. Amelia was at a party given for the gallery students, and when I saw her I realized that here was the body I had been looking for all my life. She was a crushed little thing, and I could hardly get a word out of her. Even the brandy did not make her effusive, just sleepy and sad. It was not until I had laid siege to her for many months that she let me get closer. It was a heartbreaking thing when I finally discovered why she was not the virgin which her bearing and manner led me to expect.' Paolo finished his pasta and gulped more wine.

'Imagine forcing a child! Her father was a monster and I am profoundly glad that someone has seen fit to remove him from this world. It was not, however, me. I am going to marry Amelia and remove her from that house of sorrow and she will grow fatter and happier and have many children. She loves children. I, also. I must show you the figures I did of her protegés. *Scugnizzi,* street-children, one and all, but the vitality of those undernourished bodies! And another thing. Have you seen her portraits?'

'Yes,' said Phryne, laying down her fork. 'I just bought an armload of them.'

'Then you must have seen, *bella*. You are a lady of taste and refinement. She has a great gift. She needs to do more work, her lines are still uncertain and her colour needs developing, but she can catch a likeness. Only one in three hundred students has that skill. She will be very good, when she gets away and comes to live with me.'

'What about your family? You are a Roman Catholic, aren't you?'

'This is not an impediment. I have spoken to Father John. She will become a Catholic, and thus avoid eternal damnation which she would not like. Then we shall be married in the Church. I, in turn, will renounce the delights of my models, once we are married. Thus it is fortunate for me that you came to me when you did, for I shall always remember you, *bella*.'

'I will also remember you, Paolo, *carissime*. Have you any idea who could have killed McNaughton?'

Paolo shrugged eloquently.

'It could have been anyone. But I think that it is Bill the brother. Him I do not admire. He is too much like his godforsaken father. I can see him hitting his father over the head with a rock; yes, certainly.

'Otherwise, *bella*, the possibilities are endless. He tortured his wife, and she has a secret lover. I do not know anything about him, but I assure you that there is one. I overheard her speaking to him on the telephone. "No, dearest," she said. "It is too dangerous. He will kill you. There is no hope for us," she sighed, and hung up the receiver. Her sigh would have broken your heart, *bella*. It seemed to contain all the sorrow of the world. Then she turned and saw me and begged me to say nothing. Naturally, I agreed.'

'Did you tell Amelia?'

'Of course not. She had enough to bear. But what a man, this McNaughton! Everyone hated him. His servants loathed him. He dismissed his driver recently, and beat him and kicked him into the road. He might have crept back and laid an ambush. In any case, *carissima*, it was a good deed and I hope that you do not find who did it.'

'I have to get Bill out of trouble, Paolo. Therefore I must find out who did it.'

'It is a sad world,' said Paolo portentously, 'when one who does Australia a signal service must suffer for it. Here is Guiseppe with the fish. You will like this, *bella*, it is a

126

Neapolitan recipe. Did you say that you hope to get the brother Bill out of jail? Then perhaps I should take Amelia to my studio. He does not like me.'

'You shall go and comfort Amelia. She needs you badly,' stated Phryne, taking another glass of wine. 'I shall deal with Bill. I promise that he will not say a word.'

Paolo took up her hand and kissed it.

The fish was highly spiced, and Phryne was feeling more than a little tipsy. She ordered strong black coffee and it came with a glass of cold water. She nibbled small almond biscuits and surveyed the room.

There was a shriek of recognition before Isola hurled herself across the café and threw herself into Phryne's arms.

'*Carissima!* It has been centuries. And Paolo, my dearest. How do you come to be here together? Aha! Paolo, you wicked goat, you have been seducing my friends again.'

Paolo grinned. 'How could I resist, when all your friends are so like you?'

Isola slapped playfully at his cheek, and missed. Phryne, finding Isola something of an armful, deposited her on a chair brought by a waiter, who winked. Phryne should have guessed that Isola had captured Paolo. She had a supernatural talent for finding skilful lovers. Sometimes they came in odd shapes, but if they had been Isola's choice they could be relied on to be worth the trouble. She had been honing her instincts on Melbourne men for some years.

'How is the poor Amelia?' demanded Isola, tossing back her thick tangled hair. 'I heard of the death of her disgusting father. I suppose that it was not you, Paolo?'

'No, I regret.'

'Pity. I was intending to kiss the murderer soundly.'

'It is a sad loss to me,' murmured Paolo. 'But I did not do it, Isola. Amelia, it appears, is fairly well. Tomorrow I go to her. Phryne has taken over the investigation.'

'Phryne, if you find him I shall be seriously displeased,' announced Isola in her deepest, throatiest voice.

'I shall be desolated,' said Phryne politely. 'What is that dress, Isola? You must be freezing.'

'It is the mode *Égyptienne*. Is it not seductive?' Isola stood up. She was clothed in a long, white, closely pleated gown. A collar of bright turquoise beads covered her shoulders, and her magnificent breasts lifted the fabric so that it fell uninterrupted to the floor. She looked like a lewd Corinthian

128

column. She certainly looked seductive, but Isola would have looked seductive in gunny sacks tied with old rope.

'Is this new?'

'But certainly. Have you not seen the illustrated papers? There have been great discoveries at Luxor. They have found the tombs of many Kings, and in them linen and jewellery and many fine objects. Everyone knows about Luxor! Even the children are playing pyramids. Madame *le Modiste* in the building where I live made this for me, provided that I wore it into society. I am the first, but there will be many others. Do you like it, Paolo?'

'Magnificent. I would like to sculpt you. To capture the smoothness and lightness of the fabric, while suggesting the body underneath, presents a fascinating problem. Come and model for me and I shall essay, Isola. If your current lover does not object.'

'Him? Pah! I have discarded him. He demanded that I leave the stage and go and become a good wife. Me, I have sung for Princes. But I have no time to sit for you, carissime at the moment.'

Glancing hungrily at one of the waiters, she floated away.

Paolo shrugged again.

'Ah, that Isola! The only woman I have ever met who looks on love in the same way as a man.'

'Still, her judgement is to be trusted,' observed Phryne. 'And you have to admit that she is magnificent.'

'Assuredly. She has always been so. The gown, that *Égyptienne* gown, I shall obtain one from the modiste and sculpt Amelia. I shall call on the woman tomorrow and have the gown and some clay sent to the house. Amelia likes sitting for me, it calms her. My mind is clear, now that I have completed the nymph.'

'Are you selling it?' asked Phryne. Paolo shook his head. 'I am collecting sufficient pieces for an exhibition. There, *bella*, you may buy if you wish.'

'I will look forward to it,' said Phryne. 'And now I must go. I have to be at court tomorrow. I shall see you again, Paolo.'

'At the house of McNaughton,' agreed Paolo, standing up. Phryne paid Guiseppe the surprisingly small total and took herself wearily home.

There had been no word about Candida. Jack Leonard was running out of what he had previously thought was an endless fund of aeroplane talk. Molly had gone upstairs to feed baby Alexander, and now sat rocking him and dropping tears on the upturned face. The baby resented this and did not suckle freely. Henry Maldon started when the telephone rang and snatched it from the receiver.

'Yes?'

'Henry Maldon?' whispered an androgynous voice. 'Yes.'

'We've got your little girl. She'll be fine if you sit tight and don't call in the police. A letter will arrive tomorrow. Carry out the instructions and you will have her back unhurt. Call the cops or try anything, and you'll have her back in little pieces.'

'I won't call the police,' gasped Henry. 'Is she all right? Let me speak to her.'

'Tomorrow,' promised the voice, and there was the final click of a breaking contact. Henry threw down the phone and swore.

'Was that them?'

'Yes, Jack. They say that we have to wait for a letter. Oh, Jack, how am I going to tell Molly? And how are we going to bear it?'

'You can bear most things,' said Jack. 'You're a brave man. What about the time you walked out of the Sahara?'

'That's different,' snapped Henry. 'That

131

was only me. This time, it's Candida.'

Haggard with exhaustion and strain, he poured another whisky. It was going to be a long night.

CHAPTER SEVEN

Wrest once the law to your authority
To do a great right do a little wrong
The Merchant of Venice, Shakespeare

The Melbourne Magistrates' Court was cold and stony, and Phryne was not feeling very well. The crowd of solicitors did not elevate her mood. All men, it appeared. She caught sight of Jillian across the depressing courtyard and struggled through the press of suits to catch her by the arm.

'Ah, Phryne, I have spoken to the prosecutor and he has no objection to bail with reporting conditions. The informant is our old friend and he hasn't any objection either. I just have to go in and get the matter on and we should have Bill out in two ticks.'

Phryne caught sight of Detective-inspector Benton, and called to him. He ploughed through the crowd toward them.

'Miss Fisher! How is the detecting?'

'I still have much to learn. Thank you for not objecting to bail. Tell me, can I see the body? And can I have a look at the murder weapon?'

'What will young ladies take up next? Very well, Miss Fisher. Come over to my office once you have regained possession of your client and I will show you the weapon. You can't see the body, I'm afraid, but you can read the Coroner's Report if that will do.'

'It will indeed,' said Phryne, pleased. She really did not like corpses much. She pushed her way into Court One and saw that Jillian Henderson was on her feet. She looked as plump and self-confident as the city pigeons outside, and as sure of her place.

'If I might draw the Court's attention to the matter of McNaughton, your Worship?'

A very old magistrate found his glasses, focused them on Jillian and smiled thinly.

'Yes, Miss Henderson?'

'A bail application, your Worship. I have spoken to the informant and the learned prosecutor and I believe that they have no objection.'

'Is that the case, Senior-sergeant?'

A huge policeman scrambled to his feet.

'Yes, your Worship. The informant agrees that there is no reason why the accused should not be bailed.'

'Very well, Miss Henderson; now all you

have to do is convince me.' The magistrate leaned back in his chair and shut his eyes.

Phryne was close enough to hear the prosecutor mutter: 'Damn the old cuss! This'll take all day.'

He sorted his notes, looking for the details of the crime.

'This is an alleged murder, your Worship. The victim was my client's father. The evidence against him can be summarized in three points: Firstly, he had a violent argument with his father. Secondly, he cannot be proven not to have been at the scene of the crime when his father died. Thirdly, he is very strong, and the crime required strength. For want of better evidence, your Worship, I shall be moving that the matter be struck out at Committal. For the moment, your Worship, even supposing that my client did kill his father, which is strenuously denied, there is no point in keeping him in custody. In your Worship's vast experience, your Worship must have seen a lot of domestic murderers. They do not repeat their crime. I may add to this that my client is a man of unblemished reputation with no criminal record. He has never come to the attention of the courts before. He is willing to surrender his passport and offer a surety and agree to whatever reporting conditions your Worship considers proper. As your Worship pleases...' Jillian sat down. Phryne was impressed. So, evidently, was the magistrate.

'Yes, well, I see no reason not to accede to your request, Miss Henderson. Stand up, accused. You are bailed on your own recognizance to appear at this Court on the 17th of August 1928, at ten of the forenoon, and not then to leave the precincts of the Court until the matter has been dealt with according to law. You are required to report to Carlton Police Station between the hours of nine in the morning and nine at night every Friday until the date of your hearing. Should you fail to report or appear or otherwise breach the conditions of your bail a warrant will be issued for your immediate arrest and you will have a further charge to answer in addition to those already preferred against you. Is that clear?'

'Yes, sir,' muttered Bill.

'Does your client agree to the terms of his release, Miss Henderson?'

Jillian leapt to her feet.

'He does, your Worship.'

'Take him down, usher. Accused, you will be detained until you sign your bail notice, and then you are free to go.'

Jillian and Phryne left the court.

'This way, and we'll collect Bill. Golly, Phryne, that was easier than I expected. Old Jenkins must be tired. Usually it takes a good hour of solid argument to persuade him to let anyone out of police clutches.'

She led Phryne out of the court building and along the street to the watchhouse. It was a grimy building that smelt of despair and carbolic in roughly equal proportions. Phryne hated it instantly.

'Yes, it does pong,' agreed Jillian, having noticed Phryne's grimace. 'And you never get used to it, somehow. Good morning, Sergeant. How are you this bleak and miserable Wednesday?'

'I've been better, Miss Henderson. Have you come for McNaughton?'

'I have, so hand him over – surely you don't want to keep him?'

'Not particularly,' replied the desk-sergeant, a gloomy individual with a long, drooping face. 'I'll see if they've finished with him.'

He was gone for ten minutes. He returned with Bill and the bail notice.

'Please check your belongings, sir, and sign this if they are all correct.'

Bill, who was shaky and subdued, checked

his hat, keys, wallet, cigarette case, lighter, miscellaneous coins, and spark-plug.

He signed. The copy of the bail bond was ceremonially folded and placed in an envelope. Phryne was close enough to Bill to feel him quivering with impatience.

'Steady,' she murmured. 'We shall be out of here soon.' She laid a hand on his arm as though he might bolt. Jillian, on the other side, did the same. Bill contained himself until they were out in the street again. Once there, he drew in long breaths of comparatively clean, cold air.

'My God! I need a drink. Come on ladies – the Courthouse Hotel.'

Although the Courthouse was not an ideal hotel for ladies, neither Phryne nor Jillian demurred. Bill offered both of them an arm and almost ran across the street into the comfortable beery snug, where he ordered a jug of beer. Phryne had gin and Jillian tonic water, as she had a conference in the afternoon and did not want to breathe all over the client.

'They lose confidence,' she explained, 'if you stink of alcohol. It's a dry profession,' she added. Bill had not spoken since the beer had arrived. He had been supplied with a glass but he disdained it. Lifting the jug effortlessly he engulfed the drink in a seemingly endless gulp. When he lowered it, the jug was half empty.

'Miss Fisher, I didn't kill my father.'

'I know. This is Jillian Henderson, a dear friend of mine, who has undertaken your defence.'

'Pleased to meet you, Miss Henderson. You certainly did a job on that old magistrate. He was giving the other applications a very nasty time indeed. I was surprised to see you, but I'll be delighted if you'll manage my defence.'

Here was an alteration. Three days in jail had humbled Bill McNaughton most impressively. Phryne called the barman and ordered another jug.

He brought it, and set it down in front of Bill.

'This one's on the house, mate. Boss says you're a great advertisement for his brew.'

Bill laughed, finished the first jug, and then grew solemn again.

'If I didn't kill him – and I didn't – then who did?'

'That's what I'm trying to find out. All I need from you is an exact description of the two people you saw on your walk.'

'I think you'll do this better on your own.

Let me know, Phryne. Don't forget to report, Mr McNaughton, or we may not be so lucky next time. Bye,' said Jillian and zoomed off to free more birds from the constabulary cage. Bill looked after her.

'Miss Fisher, I feel like the prodigal son. I would have been better off with the swine and the husks. Do you have any idea of what a place like that is like?'

'I once spent a night in a Turkish prison. It sounded and felt like the depths of hell and there were bedbugs.'

'Yes, that is it. The depths of hell with bedbugs. I'll do anything to avoid going back there. I say, that woman is hot stuff in court, isn't she? You could see that the magistrate was pleased. She didn't waste a word. Would it be all right if I sent her some flowers? I could have kissed her, but I didn't think that she'd like that.'

'Here is her card. I'm sure that she would love some flowers. Now drink up. Before you go back to your mother's house for a long bath, a bed with sheets and a proper shave, there are a few things I need to tell you.

'Amelia is a very good artist. She will be great. Therefore, I would have you pay her the proper respect. There is an uncertainty in her work which I attribute entirely to you. Yes?'

'She really is good? I never really looked at her stuff. Father scoffed at it so I didn't bother. Very well. I'll not tease poor Amelia. An artist, eh?'

'Here. This is a portrait of your father.'

'It's caught the pater perfectly. Who did it?'

'Amelia. I bought it from her.'

'Lord, really? Amelia?' He took a gulp of beer.

'And another thing. When you get home you will probably find Paolo Raguzzi there. You will not call him a greasy little dago. You will be nice to him. He is not only a good sculptor but he loves your sister truly and ... er ... fairly faithfully and she needs his support. He will probably want to model you; if so, you will agree. In return I will get you out of trouble.'

'You'll find the murderer if I do my Angel of the House and don't upset the mater?'

'Yes.'

'Deal,' said Bill promptly.

'The people who passed you on the path. What did they look like?'

'The first was an old man, a tramp, with a battered old felt hat and a sugar sack over his shoulder. I didn't see his face. The girl was a pretty young slip, in a red bathing-costume and cap. I couldn't see her hair but she was tanned and small – maybe five feet tall. I seem to have seen the girl before, but not the old man.'

'Any smell?'

'Smell? What do you think I am, a blood-hound? None in particular.'

Phryne wondered again at the noseless-ness of man.

'Had the girl been in the water?'

Bill absorbed more beer and thought deeply.

'Yes, her costume was sticking to her body, and her arms and shoulders were shiny.'

'Did you get the impression that the old man and the girl were connected?'

Bill thought some more and finished the beer.

'I didn't notice, really. I was in a rage. I often run down to the river and go for a quick swim when things get too personal at home.'

'I thought you were going to the aero-drome for your arguments in future.'

'Yes, I was to take the old man out there.'

'Did you kill him?'

Bill looked Phryne in the eye and said solemnly, 'No, I wish I had. Then I wouldn't mind being charged.'

'All right, Now, I shall see you into a taxi.'

'No fear! I'm going to walk. I need to stretch my legs. I will behave, Miss Fisher. I just hope you can get me out of trouble.'

She watched him stride off down the street in the direction of Kew. She crossed to the police station to find Benton and the murder weapon.

She was directed to his office and sat down while he fetched the rock from the safe.

'Can't have important clues lying about. See,' he said, opening the grey cardboard box and exhibiting a squarish block of bluestone. 'It was brought down with great force. Much more than any woman could muster. There's blood and matter on the obverse, but none on the back, indicating the blood did not spurt. The murderer might not have had a spot on him. Seen enough?'

Phryne looked very carefully at the sides of the stone, and especially the blotch of blood on the striking face.

'Doesn't that bloodstain fade toward the middle? Have a look. There seems to be less blood in the centre than you would find at the sides. What could cause that, do you think?

Benton came to look.

'No, I can't see that, Miss Fisher. Is that all?'

'Was there anything on the stone apart from blood and brain?'

'Hair, Miss, a clover burr, a few hemp strands, a few leaves, a bit of bubblegum. Nothing important.'

'No. Thank you, that was most interesting.'

'Here's the Coroner's Report. Cause of death: massive head injuries.'

Phryne skimmed through the report. 'Body of well-nourished middle aged man ... cleft cranium...'

'It seems to have fallen on the top of his head rather than the back,' she observed.

'Depends on how you look at it. Now I think he was donged from behind. The fact that the rock is a flat surface makes it difficult to say. The cranium is quite cloven through the middle.'

'Hmm. Well, thanks a lot. Have you found those witnesses yet?'

'No,' muttered the detective-inspector, straight-faced. 'Thank you so much for your time,' said Phryne politely, and left.

She sat in the car and wrote a hasty note to Bert and Cec, then drove to Canton to drop it into their boarding-house. She wondered what Bert would do when Cec got married at the end of the year, and decided that he would manage. Cec's intended was a sensible young woman who understood the bond between the two men. There would be no separating Bert and Cec this side of the death which they had so often faced together. They were skilled, if rather direct, investigators and Phryne left her problem in their hands with a certain relief.

She arrived home very tired and ate the lunch served to her by Mrs Butler with relief. A telephone message in Dot's neat schoolgirl hand informed her that Paolo was with Amelia, that Mrs McNaughton was as well as could be expected and that Bill had arrived and was behaving like an angel. Phryne decided that she had done enough detecting for one day, and went to take a long hot bath with her *Nuit de Paris* bathsalts. After that she took what she considered to be a richly-deserved rest.

Jack Leonard rolled off the couch in the Maldon's living room and strove to unkink his muscles. It had been the most uncomfortable night of his life, equalling in discomfort the Turkish brothel with the bedbugs, but without the compensating atmosphere.

Molly and the baby had retired fairly early. Molly had slept because her husband had poured a sizeable slug of chloral into her chocolate. Jack and Henry had sat up until three, when Henry had been persuaded to go to bed by Jack, who felt unequal to the strain of any more speech.

It was late in the morning; soon even Molly would be up, and no message had yet been delivered.

The Maldons trailed down to face with disgust an unwanted breakfast and it was while looking a good nourishing fried egg in the yolk that Jack Leonard had an idea. He pushed away the plate and grabbed Henry by the arm. He had just remembered something which his fellow fliers had told him.

'What you need, old man, is Miss Fisher. Top hole detective, so Bunji Ross says – brave as a lion.'

'Miss Fisher?' asked Molly, dropping her cup of tea so that it glugged down onto the breakfast-room rug.

'Certainly. High class inquiries, that sort of thing. She's been retained to get our mutual friend Bill out of trouble. I'm sure that she will be able to help. I've put good money on her getting Bill off. Amazin' record. Never fails.'

Henry seemed uncertain. His wife spoke decidedly.

'Ring her, Jack. Ring her right away.'

Phryne woke at three o'clock feeling like she had the black death. She dragged her weary body out of bed, ran another bath, and reflected that if she kept using this restorative she had better have her skin waterproofed. She felt better after her bath and decided that coffee would complete the cure.

'Oh, Miss Fisher, there is a message for you,' said Mr Butler as she sat down in the parlour. 'A child has been kidnapped and they want you to investigate. I said that I should not dare to wake you, and that you would call when you arose.'

'If it is anything like that again, Mr Butler, please wake me. Particularly if it is anything to do with a child. There are some strange people around and the first five hours are crucial. Ask Mrs B. for some coffee and get me the number, will you. Where is Dot?'

'I believe that she is in the kitchen with Mrs Butler, Miss Fisher. I shall fetch coffee at once.'

Mr B., rather abashed, gave the order for coffee and the summons to Dot, then rang the number and escorted Miss Fisher to the phone.

'Hello, Miss Fisher. Jack Leonard here. You remember me?'

'The airman, of course. What's this about a child?'

'I'm at the home of my old friend Henry Maldon. He won all that money in the Irish Lottery at Christmas, you recall. His little daughter Candida has gone missing, and we have a witness who saw her taken away in a big black car.'

'Have you a note?'

'Not yet.'

'Sit tight, Mr Leonard, and I'll be with you soon. What's the address?' Phryne scribbled busily. 'Good. Stay by the phone but don't tie it up. They might ring. Tell the parents that the child will be perfectly safe until the note arrives – then we might have to move fast. Make sure that they eat some dinner. If someone calls, try to keep them talking. Ask to speak to the child, and say that you need proof that she is alive before you give them anything. And whatever they want, agree. I'll be with you by four. Bye.'

'Dot, did you hear any of that?'

'Yes, Miss. Little girl gone missing. Terrible. Are you taking the case?'

'Of course.'

'But, Miss, what about Mr McNaughton?'

'Oh, I think I know how that happened. I just can't prove it yet. Bert and Cec will complete it. This is urgent, Dot. Get your coat and hat and come on. I might need you.'

Dot ran upstairs for her outdoor garments. Phryne drank two cups of black coffee and assembled her thoughts. The police couldn't be brought into the case officially, however there was a certain policeman who owed her a favour. She checked that she had her address book and her keys and enough cigarettes to sustain a long wait and joined Dot at the door.

'Mr B. I'm going out on a case. I don't know when I shall be back. Ask Mrs B. to leave me some soup, and just have your dinner as usual. I can be reached at this number, but only if it is really urgent.'

She was gone before he could say, 'Certainly, Miss Fisher.' He heard the roar of the great car reverberate through the house.

'She's a live wire, our Miss Fisher,' he chuckled, and went back to the kitchen.

Phryne arrived outside the new house just before four o'clock, to be met by Jack Leonard. He was not smiling.

'She really has gone,' he confided. 'We had a phone call. Not a bad little kid, Candida. And her father is an old friend of mine. I hope that you can find her, Miss Fisher.'

'So do I. This is Dot – you remember her, no doubt. All right, Jack, lead me to it.'

Molly Maldon was sitting, white as milk, in a deep armchair, staring into space. Henry Maldon was pacing up and down and seemed to have been doing so for some time. They both looked up in sudden hope as Phryne came in.

'I'm Phryne Fisher, and this is my assistant, Miss Williams. Tell me all about it.'

Hesitantly, they told her the whole story. Molly grabbed Phryne's hand.

'She's only six,' she whispered. 'Just a little girl, and she didn't even get her sweets!' She exhibited the broken bag and burst into tears again.

Candida swam muzzily back into consciousness and was immediately sick all over the car-seat and the man who was holding her. He shoved her roughly aside. She had never been cruelly handled before and she was highly intelligent. She kept her mouth shut and listened intently, although she had realized that she had been stolen and all her instincts were urging her to scream and cry and kick.

'The little brute spewed all over me,' complained the man, in a high, unpleasant voice. The woman in the front seat turned around, sneering.

'You wanted to snatch her, Sidney. You put up with it. You were the one who wanted to lay hands on all that young flesh.'

Candida did not know what this meant, but she sensed that vomiting over Sidney had removed some threat. She had done something clever. Her spirits rose a little.

Sidney was wiping at his lap with an inadequate handkerchief. It made little difference. His suit was ruined. The car stank. The driver, a big man with a bald head and a blue singlet said, 'We're almost there. Then you can hang your suit out to dry and have a bath. How about that?'

Candida liked this man. He had a deep and soothing voice. She wondered how long they had been driving. She thought that it was no use asking and that the pose of unconsciousness might be useful. She was feeling better, but she had lost her sweets, and her daddy did not know where she was. She racked her brains. What had she read about these situations? The Grimms fairy-tale method would not work. She had nothing to drop, and she could not reach the window. It began to look, she thought dismally, as though she might die like the babes in the wood, when the birds came and covered them with leaves.

The car turned off the main road. There were bumps, and the driver cursed. Then the car stopped and Candida was carried into the fresh air. Sidney was still swearing behind her.

'Did you have the note delivered?' asked the woman in her thin, whining voice.

'Yair, I sent it by reliable hands with her hair-ribbon. We'll get the dough, all right. Now carry the poor little thing inside and give her a drink and a bit of a clean-up, Ann. We're home.'

Bert collected Phryne's note and read it aloud to Cec.

'She says, "Dear Bert and Cec, I have several things which I would like you to do, for the usual rates. Find the old man and the young woman who were climbing the cliff path in Studley Park at about four o'clock on the Friday of the murder. Try the local police station – the old man is probably well known in the district. The girl is a local who was swimming in the river. When you have found them, see if they remember Bill, and then take them around and see if they know him. If they do, we are more-or-less home and dried.

"'Then I want you to search the bush and ground just outside the McNaughton home for a worn hemp rope. It will probably be about five or six feet long, and I'm hoping that it has blood on it.

"'Next, ask around for the local head kid. Find out what their favourite game was the week before the McNaughton murder. Please also collect for me all the illustrated papers for the last three weeks. Don't forget the *Illustrated London News*.

"'Last of all, scour the area for a place where they are replacing the gutter. McNaughton was killed with a large bluestone pitcher, and I want to know where it came from. It looked like a gutter stone to me. I rely on your intelligence and discretion. Don't tell anyone what you are up to if you can avoid it by any means short of prison. Best regards and get your finger out. I need this stuff as soon as I can get it. Phryne Fisher. PS. A description of the girl and the old man is attached, and here is a few quid for expenses. PF.'"

Bert shook his head.

'Where do we start, Cec?'

'At the beginning, mate,' replied Cec easily. 'At the beginning.'

The doorbell rang in the Maldon house, and Henry raced for the door. He returned with an envelope in his hand. 'No one there,' he said. 'But this letter.'

'Handle it by the edges,' said Phryne. 'Slit the top. We don't want to spoil any fingerprints, do we? Good. One sheet of cheap Coles' paper enscribed by someone who is not used to writing.

'"Dere Mr Maldon," she read, "we have yore dorter. Here is her ribon. We want five thou. Leave it in the holow tree stump in the Geelong Gardens tonite. You shal have her bak tomorow. The tree stump is on the left of the path, next to the band rotunda. A frend."'

She shook the envelope and a blue Alice band fluttered out. Henry Maldon took it into both hands as if it was the Host and kissed it gently.

'Right, produce the money and let's get cracking.'

'I can't,' said Henry simply. 'I don't have any money. I've spent it all. I bought two

154

houses and a plane and an annuity. I can sell them but it will take time. And meanwhile...

'Candida will be fine,' announced Molly, refreshed by an hour in the uncomplicated company of baby Alexander. 'About now, I bet they are wishing they hadn't taken her.'

Henry forced a small and rusty laugh.

Candida had been washed and clothed in an old white nightgown, and had accepted some bread and milk. She was as wary as a small animal and kept as far as possible from Sidney who now regarded her with loathing. The big man, Mike, was nicer. He had a large and commanding presence. The woman, Ann, she hated. After a small altercation about the nightgown, which was much too big for her, Ann had slapped Candida across the face. It was the insult rather than the pain which caused the child's eyes to follow Ann round the room with a black, implacable gaze. At last, as always, the glare made itself felt.

'Stop looking at me like that, you little toad!' shrieked Ann. Candida regarded her coolly.

'How do you want me to look at you?' she asked, imitating her mother's most infuriatingly logical voice. 'I shall not look at you at all, if you like,' she went on generously. Ann went to Mike and leaned on his shoulder.

'Make her stop looking at me, Mike,' she fawned. The child gave her a disapproving glare. Mike smiled.

'If you don't stop glaring at me, I'll tell Mike's spider to crawl right off his chest and come and bite you in your sleep,' threatened Ann. Candida was interested. Her fascination with insect life had often got her into trouble. No one had let her forget about her snail collection, which she had put down by the kitchen stove so that they could be cosy in the night. The snails had had a different idea of comfort and had glided away, some of them getting as far as the baby's room. Alexander had eaten one and Mummy had been very angry.

She got up from her seat on the hearth and disposed her nightgown around her feet. She looked up at Mike with a charming smile.

'May I see the spider on your chest?' she asked politely. Mike laughed.

'She's got guts, anyway,' he commented. 'Do you like spiders?'

'Yes. I have thirty-seven at home. Black ones,' elaborated the child calmly.

Mike stripped off his singlet and Candida

edged closer, fascinated. The spider would have covered the span of both her hands. It was impressively hairy with little red eyes. Mike took a breath and flexed his pectoral muscles, and the spider wriggled.

Candida clapped her hands.

'Do it again,' she chuckled. 'Make the spider dance again!'

'It's time for you to go to bed,' snapped Ann, and grabbed the child's wrist in a grip like a handcuff. Candida resisted.

'I have to take my asthma medicine,' she stated. 'And then say my prayers, and I cannot go to sleep without Bear. Where is he?'

She scanned the blank faces before her and her temper, never under the best of control, broke. She had lost her lollies and Daddy and Mummy and it was too much that she should have lost Bear, as well.

Mike saw her face empurple, and her body swell.

'I want Mummy and Daddy and I want my lollies and I want Bear!' she shrieked in a full-throated operatic soprano. She continued to scream until she began to cough, and then to choke. She doubled over, gasping, and a dreadful wheeze was forced from her lungs as she hauled in each breath.

'She's having an asthma attack – my sister

gets them,' said Ann. 'If we don't get her medicine, she could die.'

'So what. We don't need her alive any more,' snarled Sidney. Mike felled him with a weighty cuff around the right ear.

'Say something like that again and I'll take the girl and go straight to the cops. Now shut up and let me think. We can't call in a doctor. Where's the nearest chemist?'

'Geelong. I'll find one,' offered Ann. 'I can be back in an hour.'

'Go,' agreed Mike. Candida heard the car start. She had learned two interesting things. One was that Mike did not really have his heart in this kidnapping and the other was that they were half-an-hour from Geelong. Candida's mind was clear – she was used to asthma attacks. She was in pain but she could still hear. The other two obviously thought she could not.

'Why did you choose this place, Sid?' asked Mike.

'It's nice and quiet. No one comes to Queenscliff in the winter. It's near Geelong for the pick-up and once we have the dough all we need to do is continue along the road to Adelaide.'

Candida wheezed loudly and both men looked at her. She grimaced with pain and turned away from them.

'I wish Ann would get a move on. The poor little thing will be turning up her toes and then bang goes our chance of five thousand quid. And it's murder, too. We'll swing for it.'

'You take your chances in this game,' sneered Sid. Mike made a move towards him, then froze. Sid produced a pistol.

'I didn't know you had a gun,' muttered Mike. 'I thought we said no guns. They only get used. Put it away. I'm not going to hurt you. So what's the plan for the pick-up?'

'I'll take the car and pick up the money. If we decide to loose the kid we just set her down in the main street. She can find plenty of help. We take off to Adelaide, then you give your share to your wife, and I take a boat. There's still three warrants out for me in Victoria, and the cops would love to get their claws into me.'

'Yair, I know. I never thought I'd have sunk so low as to work with a child-molester.'

'You shouldn't have married a moll who gets you into debt then. And who is dumb enough to borrow from Red Jack. He'll break her arms and legs if she don't get him the money.'

'I know,' said Mike gloomily. 'But she likes

pretty things, clothes and shoes and I can't afford to buy 'em for her.'

'And you're afraid that she'll go off with someone who can if you don't come up with the mazuma?'

Mike made the same angry, arrested movement. Candida coughed.

'Here, you sit up, little girl,' said Mike, shifting her clumsily to lean against his arm. 'Would you like a drink?'

Candida shook her head. She did not have enough breath to drink. She tugged at the tight strings of the nightgown. Mike loosened them and fetched an old pillowcase to wipe her face. Candida hooked one arm around his neck and laid her hot cheek against the spider tattoo. Mike held her very carefully, as though she might break. He could feel the massive effort which each breath cost the child and the strain and trembling in all her muscles.

'Sid, go and get us a blanket,' he ordered, disregarding the gun in Sid's hand. Such was the power of Mike's personality that Sid obeyed. Mike unlatched Candida long enough to wrap her closely and then resumed his place. She cried after him like a puppy if he moved. He had not known that children were like this; intense in their loves and hates, and very brave. Mike admired courage. He sat like that for a long time.

At last there was the sound of the car, and Ann slammed back into the house. She put a bottle of foul, red medicine on the table and rummaged for a glass in the unfamiliar kitchen.

'I had to wake the chemist up,' she said. 'And he charged me three-and-six for the stuff. I hope it works. Here, girlie, drink this.'

She shoved the glass at Candida and the child turned her face to one side. Mike pushed Ann away.

'Let me do it. Here you are, Candida. Here is the medicine, and soon you will have Mummy and Daddy and Bear and the lollies...'

Candida drank the mixture. She was sure that they had given her double the usual dose. It tasted just as disgusting as usual. She leaned back on Mike as though he was a chair, and began to control her breathing. The adrenalin and ephedrine in the elixir had their effect. She paled to the whiteness of marble, and her lips and fingernails took on a bluish tinge. Mike thought that she looked like a tombstone angel. The wheeze faded and she accepted a drink of hot milk grudgingly prepared by Ann. At last she could speak again. She snuggled against the big man and looked up at him accusingly. 'You didn't plan this very well, did you?'

CHAPTER EIGHT

Sister Anne, Sister Anne, do you see the
horsemen coming?
Bluebeard, Charles Perrault

It was time for Phryne to call in the debts
that were owed her after the affair of the
Cocaine Blues. Thus she found herself in an
office the size of a cupboard sitting opposite
Detective-inspector Robinson. He looked
quite pleased to see her – 'Call me Jack, Miss
Fisher, everyone does' – and offered her a
cup of tea. Phryne had tasted police-station
tea before, but accepted it anyway.

'Well, Miss Fisher, what have you been up
to? My colleague, Benton, has been quite
terse about you.'

'Oh, has he? Is the man stupid, or just
very, very stubborn?'

'I wouldn't call him stupid. He's a good
detective. He just has theories, that's all.
And when he has a theory nothing will turn
him off it. They even call him "Theory"
around here. He's not a bad chap, though

163

we don't see eye-to-eye about a lot of things, one of them being you. I told him to take you seriously or risk public embarrassment, but he wouldn't listen. If you want a really biased opinion of old Theory, ask WPC Jones. He told her he didn't approve of women in the police force when she went to get her Gallantry Medal from the Chief Commissioner.'

'Gallantry Medal? I must congratulate her. What for?'

'She was acting as bait for a rapist. We didn't know that he had a knife – dirty, great cane-cutter. He got Jones down and was about to cut her throat when she rolled out from under him, stepped on his wrist and threw the weapon away; then she dropped on his chest, handcuffed his hands and feet together, and told him what she thought of him. Poor bloke. He was begging us to take him to a nice safe cell by the time the patrol caught up. A lovely job and he was lucky that she is a restrained lady, or she might have cut his balls off which was what she was threatening to do. Jones has not liked Theory Benton since. You can't blame her. He's an irritating man. Still if you come up with overwhelming evidence I'm sure that you'll give him a chance to make a manly confession, before you drop him into the soup.'

'Of course, but I don't think it will do the slightest good.'

Phryne sipped her tea, and placed the cup back on the desk. She produced the kidnap note in a larger envelope.

'Is this what you want me to do?' asked the detective-inspector resignedly. 'I didn't really think you had come just to see me and to drink police-station tea.'

'Good, because I haven't. When we were mutually involved in that cocaine affair, you were telling me that you could sometimes get fingerprints off paper. Could you have a go with this? And tell me whether they are on record?'

'I expect that I could. What's the paper?'

'A ransom note. Another thing. A big black car, probably a Bentley, and I have most of the licence number. Can you tell me who owns it?'

'How much of the number?'

'The first two digits and the two letters.'

'Yes, I can do that. But will I?'

'If I ask you very nicely and throw in a solution to the McNaughton murder?'

'We already have a solution to the Mc-Naughton murder.'

'The real solution – and a gang of kid-nappers,' offered Phryne. Robinson leaned forward.

'Kidnapping is dangerous to investigate and usually ends in the victim getting killed. If you allow that to happen my name will be mud and I will personally prosecute you for interfering with the course of a police inquiry. You know that, eh?'

'Yes, Jack, I know that.'

'Has this incident been reported to the police?'

'No.'

'So it is between you and me.'

'Yes.'

'And you are confident that you can find the gang and wrap the whole thing up neatly?'

'They shall be delivered to your door in a plain brown wrapper.'

'And you need my help, eh?'

'Yes. If you would be so kind.'

'Right, then, we know where we stand. All right. I trust you, Miss Fisher. Is there anything else that you need?'

'Not at the moment.'

'Good. Perhaps you'd like to have a word with Jones, you'll find her in Prisoner Reception this week. Give me an hour. If the stuff is on file, I'll find it,' Jack said. Phryne shook his hand and went to look for Jones.

She found the short and muscular police-woman engaged in an argument with a prisoner.

'I tell you I had ten quid on me when they picked me up. Them thieving jacks have robbed me!' a cross-eyed gentleman was roaring. Jones had been roared at by experts and did not turn a hair.

'That's all that was in your pockets, Mr Murphy.'

'It's here,' said Phryne, tweaking the ten-pound note out of an unsavoury watch pocket. 'Be more careful in future.'

Mr Murphy thanked her in an alcoholic mumble and took his leave. Jones smiled.

'Hello, Miss Fisher, you haven't half put it across old Theory. If only you can show up the old cuss! Do you know what he said to me?'

'Yes, Jack Robinson just told me. Out-rageous. Can you come out for a cuppa?'

'My shift finishes in ten minutes, if you can wait.'

'I'll just find the Ladies. I don't think that the tea here agrees with me.'

'It don't agree with anyone. Even the drunks are complaining.'

Phryne rejoined WPC Jones, who was rather pretty when out of a uniform designed to remove all dangerous allure from the female form. She had curly hair, which Phryne had only seen severely repressed under her cap. Jones led the way to a coffee shop and ordered a black coffee.

'It's hard to sleep in the daytime, and I'm so tired I can hardly keep my eyes propped open. Thank the Lord that I change shifts tomorrow.'

'I heard about your medal – congratulations,' said Phryne, gulping down a mouthful of coffee to wash the taste of the tea away.

'Thanks, but I really didn't deserve it. It wasn't cold courage. I lost my temper with the bastard. It was lucky that I threw that knife out of reach or I might have done him an injury. That wouldn't have done my career much good. Now, tell me about Theory. I know what he thinks happened. Do you think you can bring him undone?'

'Oh, yes. I can't prove it yet. But the safe money is definitely on Bill McNaughton's innocence.'

'You made an impression on Benton – even though he is sure that no woman could outsmart him, he's uneasy. He's asked two

DI's to look at the murder weapon. I do hope you can prove him wrong.'

'There is no doubt.'

'Well, I've got to go. Thanks for the coffee, and if you need anything, just give me a call. Delighted to help,' said WPC Jones, and Phryne took herself for a walk in the Art Gallery.

She returned and found a note from Jack pinned to his desk.

'Dear Miss Fisher, there are three sets of unknown prints on the letter. The only one on record is that of Sidney Brayshaw, a child-molester whom we have been very anxious to interview. If you catch him it will warm the cockles of my Chief Super's heart (assuming he has one). The only black Bentley with those prefixes in its number plate belongs to one Anthony Michael Herbert, of 342 Bell Street, Preston. He hasn't any form. Hope this is of use. Watch your step. Jack.'

Phryne folded the note, placed it in her bag and went to reclaim her car from the urchin who was minding it. She gave him a shilling and he sped off before she could change her mind.

The address in Preston was that of a run-down boardinghouse. Phryne rang at the bell and it fell into her hand. The door was open in any case. She walked, in.

'Yes, dear? Who do you want to see?' demanded the raucous voice. The speaker surveyed Phryne's black suit, silk shirt, English felt hat and handmade shoes. A toff. The woman moderated her tone from that which she reserved for the local tarts seeking custom, to that used to address her bank manager.

'Give me that bell, dear. It always does that. I'm Mrs O'Brien. What can I do for you?'

'I'm looking for Mr Herbert.'

'Mike? Him and his missus have been gone two days, Miss.'

'Gone? What – gone forever?' Phryne felt a chill at her heart. She was relying on this clue.

'No. Just gone for a holiday. Somewhere down the coast. He's a nice bloke, Mike, but his missus is a trial.'

'Do you have an address?' asked Phryne, allowing a five pound note to appear in the woman's peripheral vision. The red eyes lit up, but the puffy face sagged with disappointment, and the cigarette in the corner of the painted mouth drooped.

'No, dear, I don't know where they are.

I'm expecting them back soon. They were going to stay with their mate Sid, that's all I know. They did mention Queenscliff. Beautiful place it is. She always had to have new things – kept him skint for years, and then he lost his job when the factory closed down. He inherited that big car from his uncle but he usually can't afford the petrol. I'll keep my ear out, dear.'

'Could I have a look at their room?' asked Phryne, idly waving the banknote. The landlady scraped a hennaed curl out of her eyes and temporized, 'Well, I don't know...' Phryne produced a ten pound note. Mrs O'Brien led the way up the stairs.

At the door, her remaining scruples came to the fore.

'You won't take anything away, will you, dear? They – might be back, you know.'

'I promise. You can stand and watch me.'

Phryne began a systematic search of the freshly painted room. The lino was new and the curtains crisp. A wardrobe, stuffed full of new clothes in the worst taste, occupied one corner. Phryne looked in all the pockets and handbags, stripped and searched the mattress, turned it over and searched all the crannies of the iron bedstead. She went through a pile of magazines and all the male clothes, and sounded the floorboards for a loose one. In all this she found no sign of the destination of Anthony Michael Herbert and his wife Ann. Then a piece of newspaper caught her eye. It had been carefully trimmed out and laid among the illustrated papers. It was the cutting from the *Herald* which announced the Maldon Lottery win.

Phryne handed over the money and asked, 'How long have they been with you?'

'Three years, dear.'

'No children?'

'No, he often said that he'd like children but she refused to have any until they could rent a house of their own. And I don't allow them here. Dirty little pests. Anything else?'

'If you remember their address, telephone me at this number. It will be worth twenty quid to you, but not after Friday. Good morning,' and Phryne left.

Sidney Brayshaw's fingerprints on the note, thought Phryne. Gone to Queenscliff with their mate Sid. This was only twenty miles from Geelong. There must be a connection. Phryne drove herself home to lunch.

Bert and Cec parked their new cab in the 'Inspector only' section of the yard and marched into the Kew Police Station with determination. Neither of them liked police. While they had escaped legal notice in the past, they both had far too many dealings in dubious property to be entirely comfortable under the gaze of constabulary eyes.

'Gidday,' Bert greeted the desk-sergeant. 'We come to make some inquiries.'

'Oh, yair?' asked the desk-sergeant with irony. 'You know, I thought that we did the asking.'

'You always that funny? You should be at the Tivoli, you're wasted in a police station. Just have a look at your daybook for Friday and give a man a go.'

'I'm not even going to ask why you want me to look at my daybook for Friday. In fact, I'm such a nice policeman that I'm going to do it. What time?'

'After four in the afternoon,' growled Bert.

'Hmm. Friday was a quiet day. Nothing much happened around that time. Except that a fetching young woman in a bathing costume came in and made a complaint.'

'The tarts often wear bathing togs in the street in this part of Kew, do they? Cec, we're living on the wrong side of town.'

'She had a good reason for her lack of attire. The old Undertaker had nicked her clothes.'

'Well, well, the things that people do. It's a criminal world.'

'Yair, luckily you haven't been caught yet. Undertaker is well known in these parts. He was in that line of business before the grog got him. Anyway, we got her clothes back. Another case solved. That enough for yer?'

'Where can we find this Undertaker?'

'Heaven. At least I hope so. Of course, it depends on the kind of life he led.'

The desk-sergeant folded his hands piously. Bert snorted.

'If you mean that he's dead, why not say so? What about the tart?'

'She, as far as I know, is still with us.'

'You got her name and address there, ain't you?'

'Wild horses would not drag it from me.'

'How about ten quid?'

'Ten quid, on the other hand, might.'

He wrote out the name and address on a piece of paper and handed it to Bert. Bert gave him the money. 'Anything else I can do for you?'

'Take a long walk off a short pier,' requested Bert and he and Cec found themselves in the yard. As they started off again, he growled.

'Only one thing worse than a clean cop,

and that's a funny cop.'

'Too right,' said Cec.

The young lady's name, it appeared, was Wilson. Her address was close to the river, but she was not at home. Bert consulted the list.

'Perhaps we should do the searching while the weather's still clear. It looks like it might rain, eh, Cec?'

Cec considered the sky.

'Too right.'

They split up, working in opposite directions. Cec found the rope. It was, as Phryne had foretold, of worn hemp, and there were dark stains at regular intervals.

'Where did you find it, mate?'

Cec indicated a pile of bluestone pitchers. They had been piled carelessly, but under them Bert found a collection of small objects – a whistle, three chewing-gum cards in the Famous Kings and Queens in British History Series, the carriage of a toy train and three rings with bright glass stones. There was a licorice block and eleven lead soldiers, overpainted with what looked like white kilts.

'What do you reckon this means, mate?'

Cec shook his head. 'Maybe some kids were building a cubby house,' he suggested. 'Do we leave 'em here?'

'Yair. Now to find where they are digging up the street. I reckon they are kerbstones, Cec. Back to the cab, mate. I reckon we have earned a drink. That's two on the list. Then we look for the kids and go back for this Wilson sheila. I hope she ain't dead, too.'

'Too right,' said Cec.

Having been placated with Mike's blue singlet tied up to make a doll which substituted for Bear, Candida had fallen asleep. Mike had lain down beside her, to protect the child from any attack, and was snoring gently. Ann looked bitterly at the smooth face of the child and Mike's peaceful countenance.

'How can he sleep at a time like this!' she snarled. Sidney was loading the gun.

'He don't have to wake up ever again,' Sidney suggested. 'All I got to do is have a little accident with this gun. Then there's only two ways to split the money and no need to release the child. She's bright. She'd be able to identify us. And I got nothing to lose. If the jacks catch me they'll hang me high.'

Ann surveyed Sidney. He was a snivelling little monster, devoid of any attraction, but he could be used. Once he had the money, what was to stop her having the same accident? Then she wouldn't have to split the money at all. The world owed her some favours. All her life she had longed for money; for furs and jewellery and luxury. Five thousand pounds could buy quite a lot of pleasure. She smiled on the detestable Sidney, who had clearly seen too many gangster films.

'All right. But first we get the money. Then we deal.'

'Think about it, honey,' said Sidney. 'It ain't an offer I'll make twice.'

You horrible little worm, thought Ann. She laid a hand on his, over the revolver.

'It's a deal.'

Candida was awake and listening. This rag thing was not Bear. She could not sleep without Bear. She kept her eyes closed.

'What's the time.?' asked Ann.

'Ten ... and it's a forty-mile drive. Better go. I'll be back as soon as I can.'

'Oh, Sidney,' crooned Ann, both hands on his shoulders. 'If you don't come back, I'll find you, and when I find you, I'll kill you. Do you understand?'

Sidney's eyes dropped. 'I'll come back, baby,' he quoted, from the last gangster movie he'd seen.

Ann grabbed her coat. 'And I'll make sure of it,' she agreed. 'Mike can take care of the kid. You ain't going nowhere without me, Sid.'

Sullenly, Sid led the way to the car. Candida closed her eyes. It was about time, she decided, that someone came to rescue her.

CHAPTER NINE

The truth is rarely pure and never simple.
The Importance of Being Earnest,
Oscar Wilde

Phryne got dressed for the long night ahead. She chose black trousers, boots, a tight-fitting cloche hat and a large, loose black wool jacket with several big pockets. As she dressed she gave Dot details of the coming adventure, and received the latest news.

'Mr Leonard rang twice. Nothing new. Miss McNaughton says that she is having her children's party on Friday. Miss, how are we going to rescue that little girl?'

'This one, Dot, we shall have to fly entirely by the seat of our pants.'

'What does that mean?'

'That I really haven't the faintest idea. Get me Detective-inspector Robinson on the phone. Here's his number. I've got another favour to ask him.'

When she had the policeman's ear Phryne said, 'If you alert the Queenscliff police to the fact that an arrest may be made in their area of a notorious criminal, and that I have your personal authority to direct it, then tomorrow might bring you good news.'

'I'll attend to it. I get so little good news in this job.'

Phryne rang off and sat down to think with the aid of a tantalus, a bottle of Napoleon brandy, and a map of Victoria. Dot, tiptoeing, withdrew.

By three in the afternoon she had come to the conclusion that her first theory had been correct. There was only one way to find out where Candida was, and that was to go home with the pick-up man. She put her small pearl-handled revolver in her pocket along with other essential supplies. A box of ammunition went into the pocket on the other side. She also carried a wad of money and a driving licence, a large bag of barley sugar, and a long light rope which she wound around her waist. She included her flying goggles and went to the kitchen to canvass Mr Butler's opinion on a matter involving paint.

She set out for the Maldon household half-an-hour later, driving the red car, and Dot failed to get a word out of her. After ten minutes, she stopped trying.

'How are they, Jack?' asked Phryne, as she stepped through the door. Jack looked at her. She was a slight figure when dressed all in black, even to the cloche which hid her hair. The only colour in the whole ensemble was the bright pink of her cheeks and the grey-green of her eyes.

'Not too good. They have been arguing about going to the police for hours now. Molly is all for it and Henry's all against it.'

'It may not be necessary,' commented Phryne. 'I have a plan. But if it doesn't work we can still call the cops. I have spoken informally to my old friend Detective-inspector Robinson. Jack, can you lay your hands on a 'bus. We need a strong, fairly light plane.'

'Well, I don't own a plane and neither does Henry. He has an order in for the new Avro, but it hasn't arrived yet. I could ask Bill.'

'Of course. Tell Bill that I need to borrow the Fokker. Tell him that I will personally guarantee that I'll buy him another if we break it ... call him now, Jack, we need the plane for tonight.'

Jack went off to telephone and Phryne opened the door into the parlour.

It bore all the signs of a day of unbearable

strain. The ashtray was piled high with butts. The air was foul with smoke and fear. Molly was drinking her thirtieth cup of tea for the day and Henry was lighting yet another cigarette. A scratch meal of bacon and eggs had congealed on its plates and had not been cleared away.

'Right, everyone pull themselves together. Buck up! You shall have Candida back by tomorrow or my name isn't Phryne Fisher – which of course, it is. Open the window, Molly. Start a nice little fire in that grate, Henry, it's cold. Is your cook here? I'll go and see her. Put all that depressing food in the chook pail. Come on, up and at 'em!'

She galvanized the couple, who had not spoken since Molly had accused Henry of failing to discipline Candida and Henry had accused Molly of crushing the child's spirit. Their voices were creaky with disuse. They stood up, flinching as muscles creaked and tendons twanged. Jack came back.

'I can go and get the Fokker any time. Where are we taking it?'

'Don't know. About forty miles to Geelong and twenty more beyond that. Take a full load of fuel because I don't know where we are going to land. Dot, can you ring Bunji Ross for me and ask her if she is free to take a little fly? Now I'm going to the kitchen. Both of you, out for a brisk walk around the block. On the double!' Molly and Henry, dazed, obeyed. Jack Leonard smiled.

'You are a wonderful girl, Miss Fisher.'

'Call me Phryne, I've been calling you Jack for days. Don't be insulted that I'm asking Bunji to fly the Fokker. I'm entrusting you with a much greater honour.'

'What's that?'

'You are going to drive my car,' said Phryne. 'Help me clean up. Nothing is more depressing than a room in which three people have spent all day worrying. Get some more wood and re-light that fire, if you please. I'll tidy ... no, Dot will tidy, she's better at it than me.'

Dot returned and reported that Bunji had professed herself delighted to assist and free for the next two days. Phryne waved a hand at the mess and Dot took off her coat and hung it on the door.

Phryne found the kitchen. The cook and the maid were sitting at the table. They had evidently been weeping for hours. The maid in particular could hardly see out of her eyes. The table was littered with the remains of lunch, or possibly breakfast, and no washing up had been done.

Phryne blew into the room like a cold South wind.

'Come on ladies, buck up. We are going to find the child and bring her back by to-morrow. Up we get, Mabel,' she hoisted the maid under the arms. 'Go and wash your face in cold water and comb your hair. What would your young man think of you if he saw you like that? Come on Cook, let's get all this cleared away and I'll help you with the washing-up. The master and mistress will be back from their walk and then you and Mabel are going out, too. Is the stove still hot? Good. I suggest something sooth-ing for a late lunch. What about a cheese omelette and a nice solid sweet?'

'Apple and coconut crumble,' said the cook, drying her eyes and stowing her hand-kerchief about her person. 'We can manage that, Miss. We *have* been giving way. It's because she's such a lovely little girl. Not an angel, she's a strong-minded little creature but very clever and very good hearted. When I had a headache she bought me two of her mother's asprin and her bear to hold.' Cook managed not to burst into tears again. She relieved her feelings by stroking the stove until it ignited with a great roar of wind in the chimney. The kettle sang and the iron skillet, uncleaned after bacon and eggs had been cooked, sizzled. Cook carried it into the scullery. She scraped the plates which Dot had brought in. Mabel returned, mopped-up and collected, drew a bucket of hot water from the stove and began to wash up.

Jack Leonard and Dot had straightened the disordered room and the fire was burning brightly. A cold and refreshing breeze blew through the open front door.

'That looks better,' commented Phryne. 'You have a natural talent for order, Dot. Ah. They are back. Go and tell Cook and the maid to take their walk. A fast walk. I want them back in ten minutes. Now, when you spoke to Bill, Jack, how did he sound?'

'Quite chirpy, really. He has faith in your star, Phryne, as do we all. Are you really going to allow me to drive the Hispano-Suiza?'

'Yes. If you damage it I'll have your guts for garters. Do not let that bother you, though, just don't drive like a demon. It won't be too difficult. At least I hope not. Now, out you go, Jack. I want you and Bill to modify a big motorcar foglight to run off the engine of the Fokker. I want it to shine straight down.'

'No car headlight will be strong enough to reveal much on the ground, Miss Fisher, unless you are intending to fly at twenty feet.'

'It doesn't have to reveal anything. It only has to be strong enough to hit the road. Off you go. Here is some money. I don't mind how much it costs, but I must have it finished before dark. You'll have to take the 'bus down to Geelong before anything interesting happens. Clear?'

'Clear,' agreed Jack. 'I say, do you really know Bunji Ross?'

'Yes, she's going to fly the plane, and I want Henry to go as her observer. We are going to track the kidnappers to their lair, and we will only have one chance, so we can't afford to mess it up. Call Bunji and ask her from me to help and advise; you'll like her, Jack, but see if you can prevent her from fighting with Bill. Tell him that on Friday I anticipate solving the murder, and he must continue to be the Angel of the House.'

Jack left. Molly and Henry returned from their walk, feeling better and Phryne asked them to show her around their house. It was new, and some of the chests had not been unpacked. Phryne decided that this would be a splendid occupation for a worried woman.

'Molly, you should unpack all these boxes. I'll send Dot to help you, she's great at putting things away. I tend to just stuff the clothes into a wardrobe. If the door shuts, I think it's all right, but Dot is neat. You stay up here and I'll send her to you. It will be all right, I promise. You have my word. We shall have her back by tomorrow. It's just a matter of getting through the time, and we can't move until tonight. Cook will bring you a light meal and I want you to eat all of it even if you are convinced that it will choke you. I need you in good shape for tonight and you will find that you are hungry after the first three mouthfuls. What a charming room. Did you choose the wallpaper?'

Molly nodded. She had been very proud of that wallpaper. It seemed like such a long time ago now that she had moved into this house in which she had hoped to be very happy. Phryne interpreted the look.

'You'll be happy here again if you can regain your sense of proportion,' she said over her shoulder. 'When I see Candida tonight I'll need some token that I am trustworthy. What would convince her?'

'Bear,' said Molly with conviction. 'She will be leading those kidnappers a hell of a dance because she hasn't got him. Come this way,' she said, and led Phryne upstairs to the nurseries. Baby Alexander had been sent on a visit to his doting grandmother. His room, decorated with bunnies all round the walls, was empty, but had a feeling of recent occupation. Candida's room was hollow. It was clear that the child who had slept in this little blue bed and worn these pyjamas and played with these toys was missing, not just gone for the day. Molly controlled herself with a great effort and snatched Bear off the bed.

Phryne retreated from the room and shut the door. There was a limit to what a stepmother could stand. She held up Bear and looked at him. He had been a proper golden plush Pooh-bear at one stage in his life, but he had been extravagently loved for some years since then, and he was a little battered. One of his ears had been carefully re-stitched, and his joints were loose. His squeaker no longer worked and the repairs to his face after some childish accident had given him a lop-sided grin. He was a Bear of great, if raffish, charm and Phryne could understand why Candida relied on his company and counsel. This might be a bear of very little brain, but even his furry body had been moulded, by the hugs of years, to fit Candida's embrace. Phryne gave Bear a brief squeeze and tucked him under her arm.

'To your boxes, woman,' she ordered Molly. 'Bear will be safe with me.'

She marched back into the parlour, where Henry had started pacing again.

'Dot, can you go and help Mrs Maldon? She's upstairs, unpacking. Talk to her about her new house, baby Alexander, and anything else that occurs to you. Don't go into Candida's room if you can help it.'

Dot obeyed. From the kitchen came the appetizing scent of an omelette cooking, and bread toasting. Henry took Bear out of Phryne's arms and hugged him. Phryne glanced at his face and went out. She decided that Bear should be left alone to work his magic.

She dialled her own house. Mrs Butler answered the phone.

'Mr Butler has got the paint you ordered, Miss, and says that what you need to deliver it is the bladder from a football. He's just gone out to buy one.'

'Good. He is a jewel among men and I hope that you are very happy with him.'

'And your two cabbies are here with a load of papers which they say you asked them to buy.'

'Good again. Tell them to wait until Mr B.

comes back and to bring the doings over to the Maldons'. Did they say if they found the rope?'

'Mr Bert is here, Miss, I'll put him on.'

Bert, who was unused to telephones, roared in Phryne's ear.

'Bert here, Miss. We got the rope.'

'Good, but keep your voice down. Was it where I said it would be?'

'Yair. Cec found it, and a pile of pitchers. We reckon they are kerbstones. We'll go out looking for the street repairs later. The rope had blood on it all right. Reckon it was used to tie someone up. The stains are all spaced out, like. And there were all these little things under the stones.'

'What sort of little things?'

'Lollies, and toys, and gum cards, and lead soldiers. Someone had painted over their uniforms and given them white skirts.'

'Ah,' said Phryne with deep satisfaction. 'Had they. Have I told you lately how invaluable you are, Bert?'

'Not lately,' said Bert, 'But I'll pass your recommendation on to Cec. Now about the old bloke and the girl – no wonder the poor sheila was chasing him up the path. He'd pinched her clothes. This smarmy cop thought it was real funny. Cost me ten squid

190

to square him. Is that all right?'

'Cheap at the price,' said Phryne. 'Come over here with the paint and the footy, as soon as you can. The game's afoot, Bert, and I'm hoping to have Candida back before tomorrow night. After that we shall see. You keep looking for the local top cocky, and the street repairs, and I'll see you soon. Bye.'

Phryne could hear Bert ask, 'What do I do with this thing now?' as she rang off.

Bert and Cec arrived an hour later in their new taxi. Omelettes and jam roll had been consumed, the household having run out of coconut, and Molly Maldon was so absorbed in telling Dot all about what a bargain her new carpet had been that she did not flinch when the doorbell rang. The two cabbies came in with the bladder and the paint, and an armload of illustrated papers. Phryne waved her scissors at them.

'Come in! I'm just cutting up five thousand pounds worth of valuable newspaper. Put them down there on the sofa,' she directed, and Bert laid down his burden. 'This is Henry Maldon, the flyer. Tell me about the funny cop.'

'Pleased to meetcher,' growled Bert, who did not approve of capitalists. He took a tense hand and shook it. Henry Maldon

191

looked much better than he had two hours ago, but there was enough residual agony in his face to make Bert revise his opinion. 'He couldn't help winning the money,' he told Cec later. 'And the poor coot looked like he'd been strained through a sieve backwards. Sitting there clutching that teddy bear. Must'a belonged to the kid.'

Bert abated his gruffness instantly and strove to amuse.

He made a good story out of the cop, and coaxed a smile out of the distracted flyer. Phryne bound her newspaper bundles with a real note on the top and bottom, and placed a bundle of real fivers on the top. The notes were packed into a cloth bag. There was a strained silence.

'Come down to the pub, mate,' offered Bert to his own astonishment. 'Man needs a beer. Still an hour before time.'

The ormolu clock on the mantelpiece said five. Phryne refrained from hugging Bert and observed, 'We can't do anything until it's dark. You go with Bert and Cec. I'll come and get you if something happens. Which pub are you going to?'

'The Railway,' said Henry, and the two cabbies took him away. This was a relief to Phryne, who had not been able to find

Henry an occupation. There was still a couple of hours to go before there was any point in setting out for Geelong.

Phryne heard the voice of the cook raised in comfortable converse with the butter-cream-and-egg man, who was late.

'What are you coming here at this time of night for?' she demanded, and Phryne heard the reply from the back yard.

'Couldn't go any faster, Missus, not even to woo me old sweetheart. The bleedin' Council have dug up the bleedin' road and I had to wheel me trike all the way from the shop. My boss is creatin'. So don't you start on me, there's a love.'

'Language,' cautioned the cook. 'And don't come smoogin' up to me. Them eggs you brought yesterday was mostly rotten.'

'What? My eggs?' exclaimed the delivery boy, as outraged as if he had laid them personally. 'My eggs, rotten? You show me a rotten egg I've delivered. You must have got 'em mixed up with them tichy little ones from your own chooks.'

'The chooks ain't laying,' returned the cook, 'or I wouldn't have to buy your rotten ones.'

'Give a man a break,' complained the boy, who sounded about fifteen. 'The boss says,

"Take them eggs", so I take 'em. I ain't got no choice. How many of 'em were off, anyway?'

'Three out of the dozen, and I had to throw away a whole cake batter with a pound of butter in it. I wouldn't have offered it to a pig. I ought to get onto your boss, however,' admitted the cook handsomely. 'I suppose that it ain't your fault. Give me a dozen more, and two pounds of butter, no cream today.'

There was a thud as the parcel was placed on the kitchen table. 'See you temorrer, my old darling,' cried the boy, and took off quickly, in time to avoid a slap.

'Not so much of the "old",' snarled the cook, and slammed the kitchen door, much invigorated.

Phryne took up the illustrated papers and leafed through them. A characteristic passage met her eye.

'The recent discoveries at Luxor have sent the whole Empire mad about Egypt,' it said smugly. 'Lord Avon, who has been largely responsible for financing the expedition, said that the public interest was most gratifying. "There is a whole civilization under the sand here," he said to our special correspondent. "And one of very high standards. The decorative patterns, the linen, the beading and the magnificent tomb painting of the Pharoah are unforgettable and as fresh as the day they were painted. I expect to find many more tombs in this area. It seems to have been a flourishing city. I also hope to find the chamber which I am convinced lies under the great Pyramid, the resting place of Cheops himself. Further interesting discoveries are expected daily.'"

She laid the magazines open at the pictures of the objects discovered in the rock chambers. A dagger inland with hunting cats. A diadem for a queen, with lotus flowers in lapis lazuli. A bracelet for an archer inland with the Eye of Horus to safeguard his aim. Tomb paintings of the Pharoah hunting lions, and mixing wine, and embracing his wife. Small figurines of gods and slaves and workmen: little women kneading dough, herding cattle, shearing sheep and reaping wheat. They were enchanting. Phryne stared longest at the gold statue of the Goddess Pasht, a graceful cat with an earring in one of her upstanding ears and kittens at her delicate feet.

That is beautiful beyond belief, thought Phryne. I wonder if I could steal it?

CHAPTER TEN

Night makes no difference 'twixt
Priest and Clerk
Joan as my Lady's as good i' the dark
No Difference in the Dark, Herrick

At last it was getting dark. Phryne packed
Dot, Molly, Jack Leonard and herself into the
Hispano-Suiza. She checked that she had all
the impedimenta that had been improvised
and collected during the day. Though she
and her hosts had eaten an early dinner they
added a picnic basket to the load, as well as
brandy flask, and of course, Bear.

'It's not all that far to Geelong but I don't
want to hurry,' she said as Jack Leonard
swung the starting handle. 'Are we clear as
to what we are going to do?'

Everyone nodded.

'Right,' said Phryne taking a deep breath.
'Off we go, then.'

She located the Geelong Road without
difficulty and soon they were bowling along
in the darkness. There would be a moon but

it had not yet risen. It was clear and frosty and the stars were very bright. Phryne hoped that she wouldn't freeze to death on the escapade which she had in mind. She had already fought a fierce action with Jack Leonard, once he heard what she intended to do.

'Don't be silly, Jack. Look at the size of you. I'm five feet three and I weigh eight stone with all these clothes and goods. How much do you weigh?'

'Twelve stone. I suppose that you are right. But what if you fall off?'

'Then you shall pick me up,' said Phryne, and the conversation was at an end.

Dot was talking to Molly Maldon to distract herself from how cold she was, how worried about Phryne, and how fast the car was going. Molly was keyed-up. After what seemed like years of hanging about and worrying, there was now a chance of some action and she was all for it. The afternoon among her possessions had soothed her spirit and she had great faith in Phryne. She was beginning to believe that she would recover Candida. She had the bag of lollies in the picnic basket, though she had an instinctive and superstitious dread of picturing how glad Candida would be to see them, and paid as much attention as she could to Dot's account of one of Phryne's previous cases.

'And this abortionist was her capture, was he?'

'No, that was a police-lady called... Miss, what was the police-lady's name, that caught that ... er ... you know, the chap that operated on women.'

Dot would not say the word 'abortionist', any more than she would swear in church.

'WPC Jones. I saw her today. She got a medal for seizing the Brunswick rapist.'

Dot could feel her cheeks burning. Everything she said seemed to have a sexual meaning.

Phryne, perceiving her embarrassment, launched into flying-shop talk with Jack Leonard.

'Did you like Bunji, Jack?'

'She's a ball of lightning, isn't she? Bustled in and spent twenty minutes with her head in the engine, and then she and Bill worked out how to mount the light. It's a drain on the power supply but I don't think it's enough to significantly affect the performance.'

'Did she argue with Bill?'

'All day. You could tell that they were both having a lovely time. And she's a sporting flyer. Took the Alps and even flew over the

Himalayas. Said that all you had to do to thoroughly depress the spirits was to look down. Nowhere at all to land – just rocks.'

Phryne laughed, and shifted into top gear.

The Geelong Road was visible only as a tarmac trail that gleamed faintly in the lights of the powerful car. There was no sound but the roar of the engine and the swish of the slipstream. Luckily Mr Butler had managed to put the hood into place or the passengers would have been even colder than they were. The stars shone down like lanterns – no, they were on the road – two swaying lights. An odd noise began to make itself heard. Phryne listened attentively. It was halfway between a clatter and a clop like hooves. She racked her memory, and concluded that she really was hearing a new sound.

'Can you hear that?' she asked.

Dot cried out, 'Slow down!'

Phryne applied the brakes and the car lost momentum. She had almost stopped when the explanation was vouchsafed to her.

A wave of advancing sheep circled the car, their fleeces oddly grey in the starlight. The moon was rising. The lanterns gleamed. A ghostly stockman, looking like a revenant from the past, raised a casual hand. Two jinkers clattered past, with bags slung underneath for the dogs to rest in. A dog barked. The sheep trotted down the road.

'Thank you, Dot, I might have ploughed right into them. I didn't know they took sheep along this road. And in the dark. How dangerous! They must be going to Borthwicks – and there's the cemetery. How convenient. Well, tally-ho, and if anyone sights a flock of flamingoes or a herd of elephants, just let me know.'

'Where are we?' asked Molly.

'About halfway I should think. We have to look out for Bunji and Henry in the Fokker outside Geelong. They should be over on the left side of the road, near the railway bridge. Give me a shout if you see them. Then we have to test the plan. I would feel very silly if I went ahead with it and it turned out not to function. I'd be left on my own with the kidnappers and they are probably armed.'

'Are you?' asked Jack. Phryne nodded.

'Certainly. But I hope not to have to use it. I do not approve of guns.'

'Good shot, are you?'

'Not particularly. At the distance one has the most use for a pistol, however, it makes no difference. A man is too big a target to miss at a range of five feet.'

'Why five feet?'

'Any closer and he can grab,' explained Phryne. 'Let's talk about something else.'

Jack Leonard obliged with a dissertation on the merits of Rolls Royce engines which lasted until they were nearing Geelong.

'They bore their engine blocks, put them out to weather in a field for two years, and then re-bore them. I have never come across a Rolls with cylinder trouble. Marvellous machines... Hello! There's the Fokker.'

Phryne swung the car off the road and drew to a halt on a flat paddock. The flying machine was stopped and had been turned on the grass so it could be got back into the air with the greatest dispatch. Bunji Ross, short and plump in her flying suit and boots, strolled over and grinned at Phryne.

'Hello, Phryne. You'll be pleased to hear that the gown was a great success. I only spilt a little tomato soup on it, which is good, for me. I've mounted the light, m'dear and I can cast a fairish light on the road, but only at very low altitude. I can't make much impression on it over fifty to seventy feet. What's the landscape from here to where you are going? Any mountains?'

'Not as long as you follow the road. Leave the road and the ground gets very lumpy away to the left. If you can keep the plane to the right of the road, you'll be fine.'

'Good, will do. I've got Henry with me. He has a good pair of Zeiss-Ikon binoculars and seems competent in the air. Come and let's give this idea a try. Run her back toward Melbourne, pet, we don't want to muddy our trail.'

Phryne dabbed a small drop of paint on the road, then took the car slowly along, dripping a little paint out of the driver's side. She continued for a quarter of a mile, then took the car off the road and waited.

Overhead, but only just overhead, the Fokker engine roared. The plane circled once above the car. She dipped her wings, and flew off towards Geelong.

'Good. It works. Bunji really is a brick. We are almost there. Jack, you take the wheel and remember what I said about garters.'

Geelong was a sizeable town, encircled by grain silos and storehouses, with a respectable townhall and wide streets. It did not keep late hours. The only person Phryne saw who seemed to be awake was a strolling policeman. Phryne took note of the moon. It was now bright and full.

'There's the park, Jack, stop for a while at that corner near those big elms. Light a cigarette and look bored. Stand there until you finish the smoke, then you can go into the park and stop short of the band rotunda. According to the map, it must be about three hundred yards over that way. Molly takes the money and puts it into the hollow stump. Don't stop and stare, just drop the bag in and walk away. Then you start the car and give her a lot of high revs in case they are already here. Then get back on the road and wait. We could be here all night, but don't go to sleep. You wait for the plane, and keep a good way behind it. You'll be able to see the light for quite a long way. In any case I think that we are going to Queenscliff. Break a leg,' said Phryne, and slipped into the darkness. In her black garb she was hard to see, and she stopped at a convenient mud-puddle and smeared her face.

The band rotunda was white wrought-iron, and it stood out under the moon like the bare ribcage and spine of a fabulous monster. Phryne waited until her eyes had got used to the light, then began to creep, sloshing slightly with her bladder of fluorescent paint, across the invisible grass.

Luckily it was not yet frosty, although it would certainly be so before dawn. She told herself that she was as good and ruthless a hunter as the Egyptian cats, and paused with one hand on a tree. She stepped into shadow, rolling her foot carefully forward from the toe: not a twig cracked under her feet. She had reached the rotunda and was about to cross the path when she saw a point of light, and heard someone whistling softly. There was a man, sitting at ease on the rotunda steps and smoking. Phryne's spirits rose. This did not look like a professional kidnapping. Of course he might not be the one – but what sane man would have been found sitting in a rotunda at midnight in the middle of winter?

She was confirmed in this opinion by his behaviour when the noise of the Hispano-Suiza was heard. He threw his cigarette away and crouched down below the railings.

Phryne also crouched. She heard the crunch of Molly's feet on the gravel and the thud as the bag dropped into the hollow stump. Molly's feet moved away again and there was the revving of a big engine.

Don't get too carried away with my car, Jack Leonard, thought Phryne. Is this my man or not? Damn him, won't he move? I'm freezing to the spot.

Sid moved at last. He sauntered over to the stump, extracted the bag, and ripped open the top. He stuffed a handful of flyers into his pocket and tucked the bag under his arm. He walked jauntily down the path toward the other side of the park and did not give the slightest thought to the shadow that moved when he did.

He was planning to go back to Queenscliff to eliminate the witnesses, not share the money. He still had five shots in his revolver. That would finish Mike, the woman sitting silently in the car, and the kid. He would leave the pistol in Mike's hand then catch a boat from Adelaide bound to anywhere, with five thousand quid in his kick. He licked his lips at the thought of the ten-year-old child slaves he could buy in Turkey, with that amount of money.

The Bentley was warm and he only needed to swing the starting handle before the engine caught. Sidney did not so much as glance at Ann as he got in and drove away.

Phryne had not had any difficulty in ensconcing her slight frame behind the rumble seat. She unwound the line from her waist and lashed herself to the back of the car, using the convenient lugs placed there for tying up luggage. Tonight, thought Phryne, he hasn't got luggage, he's got baggage. This feeble witticism amused her as she hung on when the Bentley rounded a corner. She had the bladder of paint in a sling contrived by Dot, placed on her right hip. All she needed to do to drop some paint was to give the bladder a soft thump. The excreted paint would shine on the black surface of the road as soon as the light from the plane touched it.

Phryne had not gone fifty yards before she began to curse her own cleverness. This was ingenious, but couldn't much the same effect have been obtained by tying the bladder to the car? She supposed not. She had no way of timing because she could not spare a hand to hold her watch. Bear was safe and snug against her chest. Phryne banged the bladder and a drop of paint squeezed out. She began to sing under her breath as the car whizzed along and the cold wind slashed at her hands.

She thumped the bladder at the end of each line. Observing angels would have heard had they been hovering over her in the dark:

John Brown's body lies a-mouldering in
  the (thump)
John Brown's body lies a-mouldering in
  the (thud)
John Brown's body lies a-mouldering in
  the (thump)
But his soul goes marching (thud)!

Phryne hoped that by this novel method she could space out the drops of paint so that the plane could follow them. Geelong was fleeting past. Soon they were out into the open paddocks again. The moon was high and the light bright enough for Phryne to read the engine specifications embossed on the Bentley's rear.

She was exquisitely uncomfortable. She had bound herself as tightly as Andromeda to the rock, as she did not relish being flung off into the night. Struck at thirty miles an hour, the road was sure to be very hard indeed. Her fingers, in their leather gloves, were beginning to cramp. She eased the pressure by leaning into her line, and though it took her weight, it creaked rather alarmingly. Her feet were wedged above the bumper bar, where the maker of the car had decided to make a definite little shelf about ten inches long.

The car surged up and over a hump in the road, and Phryne lost her grip. Her clawing hand met the tail light and she hung on to it as though she had been glued while she scrabbled with her feet for the step. She found it and gave the bladder a hearty thump. Geelong was now not even a glow on the skyline, and the moon was westering. Where was the plane? Had the paint failed to work? That was not disastrous.

Phryne freed a hand to scratch her itching nose and reminded herself that poor little Candida was at the end of this wild ride. If she was still alive. Phryne banged the bladder again.

The grand old Duke of (thump)
He had ten thousand (thud)
He marched them up to the (thud) of the
  hill and he marched them (thump) again.
And when they were up they were (bang)
And when they were down they were
  (slosh)
And when they were only halfway (thud)
They were neither up nor (bump)
Oh, the Grand old Duke of (thump)

Phryne began again, when she heard the buzz of a plane engine. She strained her ears, and risked a brief glance over her shoulder.

Riding up, circling majestically, the Fokker came into sight in the moon-glow, gleaming as silver as a trey bit. A faint stream of light radiated from her belly. It had worked. Phryne cheered silently, and barked her knuckles as the driver turned off the main road.

The plane was being flown by an expert – Bunji was to be congratulated. Phryne saw that the slow, sweeping circles, the most dangerous and difficult of all manouevres to attempt at night, covered the road with light while not making it obvious to the drivers underneath. They had not, as it happened, seen any other motors, as the winter attracted few people to the coastal resorts, and the locals knew better than to be out at this hour in this weather.

The road surface had worsened. Phryne kept her face pressed against the car, as the big machine spurned the stones and flung them high. One sneaked through her guard and cut her over the eyebrow. She wondered how Candida, a well-brought up little girl, would react if she had to catch her before Phryne had a chance to wash her face. Probably scream and run.

She wiped some of the blood off to clear her eyes, and then remembered that she had goggles. The struggle to extract them from her pocket, keep thumping, and not fall off in the process took her mind off the pain for five miles of gravel and a mile-and-a-half of mud.

Relieved of the fear of road gravel in the eyes, she donned the goggles and looked for the plane. It was about a quarter of a mile behind, flying as evenly as an eagle. Bunji was credited with the ability to smell the ground. The sweeping swing would have taken a less brilliant pilot straight into the deck, and it was very hard to judge how much height had been lost at the edge of each circle. The mud road was more comfortable, and Phryne prayed that they did not get bogged.

She listened for the familiar sound of the Hispano-Suiza but could hear nothing above the roar of Sid's car.

In the cockpit of the Fokker, Bunji Ross was examining her instruments by the light of a torch. Flying speed was satisfactory, they had plenty of fuel, and the moon was giving almost enough light to fly by. At the bottom of each swoop she dropped the plane to within fifty feet of the road, and waited for Henry to call, 'Got it!' before she took to the air again. The engine was running sweetly. Bunji took a swig of black coffee from her thermos and offered it to Henry.

Henry gulped the bitter brew and returned the flask. He was lying on his face with the binoculars out of the hole which Jack and Bill

210

had cut in the superstructure. Bill had not turned a hair when Bunji had announced that this was the only way she could devise of seeing out of the bottom of a plane. Hard struts dug into all the sensitive portions of his anatomy, including some which he had not known were sensitive before, but he did not care. He was on his way to retrieve the infuriating but beloved Candida.

Jack Leonard was controlling the big car with a minimum of effort. She was fleeing as softly along this dirt road as a spectre. Dot was handing out cups of thermos tea, and ham sandwiches. Jack bit into one absently. He kept the plane in the right-hand corner of the windscreen. He could not see the car which it was following, but that was according to Phryne's orders. They would not just chase along behind and be seen, or seize the pick-up man and beat him to a jelly, because of Candida. Nervous kidnappers kill their charges. Molly drank her tea and ate two sandwiches without prompting. She was half-tranced by this midnight ride on the empty road, and was possessed by the odd illusion that all the outside world was flying past, and the car was still, at the heart of the darkness.

CHAPTER ELEVEN

When in doubt, win the trick
*Hoyle's Games: Whist 24 Short Rules
for Beginners*

Bert and Cec had discovered the street repairs. Bluestones were stacked into a rough wall all along Paris St, where the workmen were replacing them with cement gutters. Several local households had helped themselves to a wheelbarrow load to construct their own rockery or a garden wall.

'This is the place, Cec. They've been here a few days, too, see, the grass is starting to grow over them. What's the last item on our list, eh? Oh, yair, the kids. This looks like a good street for kids. There's a gang of 'em now ... what have they got? A cat, is it?'

Cec was already running towards the group of five children who appeared to be tormenting a cat. Cec plucked the half-grown kitten out of their grasp and caught it under his arm so that he could examine it. It seemed to have sustained only a wounded front paw. One of the claws had been un-skilfully cut.

'Give me a bit of that rag,' ordered Cec, pointing with his free hand to a pile of bandages on the ground. One of the children, a grubby girl, burst into tears and another bit the end of her plait. The smallest urchin began to howl.

'It's all right, kids, don't go crook. We ain't going to hurt you, nor take you home to your mothers neither. We just want some information.'

Cec had bandaged the cat's front paw.

'We weren't going to hurt it, Mister, but it wouldn't keep still, and kept on scratching, so we thought we'd cut its claws. We didn't know that they'd bleed,' said a wiry little kid with a collarless shirt and knotted braces. Bert had caught up by now and was getting his breath back. The children stared at him righteously.

'We didn't know it was going to bleed, did we?' repeated the kid. Heads all nodded in chorus. The grubby girl wiped her face on a far-from-clean calico petticoat. The plait-sucking child said nothing.

'Are you the kids who play in McNaughton's?'

They nodded again. The smallest one

howled and one of the others stopped his mouth with a pre-loved rainbow ball.

'That's Mickey. He howls,' said the wiry kid. 'I'm Jim, this is Elsie,' the plait-chewer nodded. 'And Janey,' the grubby girl made a bob. 'And Lucy, she's Mickey's sister and she has to take him with her.' Lucy grinned, showing that she had not received two front teeth for Christmas. Mickey was silenced by the gobstopper.

'Listen, kids, I want some information and I'm willing to pay for it. What will it be? A deener's worth of lollies?'

Mouths watered all around the circle. Jim considered.

'That's old Mother Ellis's cat,' he said. 'We sort of borrowed it and if she finds out that we hurt its paw, she'll tell all of our mums and we'll all get a hiding. If you can fix it with Mother Ellis, and give us the lollies, it's a deal.'

Bert looked at Cec, who was cradling the cat. The cat, which was a fine midnight-black pedigreed short-hair and no doubt very valuable, had placed one paw on either side of Cec's chin and was gazing lovingly up into his eyes.

'Can you do it, mate?'

Cec nodded. Jim escorted him to the

house and watched with admiration as Cec walked straight up to the front door and banged the knocker, loud. The door opened and Jim ran for his life.

Mrs Ellis was a vicious old bitch, who punctured footballs kicked over her fence and shot at trespassing dogs with an air rifle.

She had never given back a tennis ball, either, or a kite, and the children believed that she sold them. Mr Ellis had thankfully given up the ghost twenty years before and no man who was not a relative had crossed her threshold since. The house was offensively clean and stank of carbolic. There was a trail of newspapers laid down the hall over the polished floor. The children called her a witch and her letterbox never missed its cracker on Bonfire night.

Although the house was cold as a grave, no smoke ever trailed from its chimneys. The kids believed she had the fires of Hell to warm her. She wore her thin web of hair scraped over her scalp and knotted at the back of her head, and was always dressed in black. Her face reminded Cec of a boarding-house pudding with currants for eyes.

'Mrs Ellis?' he asked in his soft warm

voice. 'I've brought you back your cat.'

The black cat turned in his embrace and stared the old woman straight in the eye, as if daring her to start something. She saw the bandage on the paw.

'What's happened to him? Have those little devils hurt him? I'll have all of their bottoms tanned if they've touched a whisker.' Her voice rose to an eldritch screech.

'The kids might have had nothing to do with it,' said Cec reasonably. 'It's only his front claw that's broken. He might have caught it in something. Does he like climbing trees?'

'Yes, he does, the varmint,' she said, patting her cat.

'And it was the street kids who put the bandage on his paw and told me where he belongs,' continued Cec, as if there was nothing in the world such as perjury. 'He'll be as good as gold after dinner and a sleep. The claw will grow again in about a month.'

'You know a lot about cats?'

'A bit,' said Cec, who had inflicted six of them on his long-suffering landlady.

'Come in,' she invited, and Cec stepped inside. The watching children gasped in chorus.

Mrs Ellis took Cec into her kitchen, where

an electric heater warmed the room. The four cats who had draped themselves over the dresser and chairs lifted their heads and pricked their ears. They were all beautiful. Apart from the midnight-black in Cec's arms, there was a tortoiseshell, a silver tabby, a mackeral tabby, and a ginger Tom. They were all well fed and groomed. The old woman went to the ice-chest and took out two jointed rabbits.

'Dinner, my dears,' called Mrs Ellis. The cats rose, stretched, and approached their food with royal leisure. Cec set the black cat down by his plate and he began to eat hungrily. Mrs Ellis stroked it with her gnarled hands, and Cec found himself close to tears. He swallowed.

'Well, Mrs Ellis, I must go. Hope that the little fellow recovers well. I'm sure he'll be bonzer in a couple of days. Your cats are beauties,' commented Cec. Mrs Ellis accompanied him to the door and thrust a penny in his hand.

'Tell them kids not to make so much noise outside my house,' she snapped, and slammed the door with less than her usual force.

Cec was met at the gate by Jim.

'She gave me a penny for you,' he handed

it over. 'She's not such a bad old chook if you leave her cats alone.'

Jim stood open-mouthed. A man invited into old Mother Ellis's house who emerges not only with his life but with a reward!

'All right,' said Jim, gathering his clan around the cabbies. 'What do you want to know.'

Bert told them the story of poor Bill McNaughton, unjustly accused of killing his father. He reminded them that on that very Friday they were going to a party with Miss McNaughton, where they would be entertained and fed. Could they take the lady's jelly and buns and ginger-beer and refuse to help her brother? Jim thought about it, and they drew off to confer. Elsie uncorked her mouth and said her first words. 'Tell them, Jim. I trust them.'

This seemed to be some sort of talisman. Bert had the whole story in ten minutes. He marvelled at the perspicacity of Miss Fisher once again, and handed over the shilling. He had just got some new change from the bank, so it was a bright and shiny shilling. The children gazed at it as it lay in Jim's hand. Unnoticed, little Mickey edged close to him and made a sudden grab.

'Quick, he'll swallow it!' screamed Lucy.

Bert, the eldest of six children acted with dispatch. He seized Mickey and turned him upside down like a chicken to be slaughtered, then gave him a hard thump in the middle of the back. Out shot the shilling. Elsie dived on it and tied it into her handkerchief. She stowed the hankie in the leg of her bloomers. Bert put Mickey down on his feet. He howled. It seemed to be his forte.

'Lost my rainbow ball!' he screamed. Lucy found it on the pavement and stuffed it back into the gaping mouth. Bert shuddered, but then reflected that children, like ostriches, seemed to be able to digest anything.

'All right, kids, we'll see you at Miss McNaughton's party on Friday. Not a word until then, eh?'

The heads nodded in a row. Bert and Cec went to reclaim their cab. A sudden thought struck Bert. He came back.

'What did you want to do to that cat?' he asked. Jim looked up from the old envelope on which he was taking orders for lollies.

He told Bert what they wanted with the cat. Bert roared with laughter.

'You're supposed to wait until they're dead!' The children blushed.

Seconds before the last of Phryne's sinews gave out, the car arrived at its destination. It stopped in a dark spot under the gumtrees. Phryne untied herself and fell backwards onto the road, before the roar of the engine died. Ann and Sidney got out of the car without noticing her, and walked into the house.

Phryne was bruised all over and her hands and feet were cramped and pinched. For a minute she lay still, unable to move, then gently she flexed and stretched until she was able to get to her feet.

There was still plenty of paint in the bladder. Lavishly, she traced a big cross on the road. A plane flew over and dipped both wings in salute.

Success. Phryne shook her shoulders and the folds of her jacket fell into place, loaded with equipment. She drew a line to the front gate of the house, and crept around it like a Red Indian tracking a particular scalp. The only light she could see came from the back of the house. She guessed it was the kitchen.

Sidney opened the front door with his key and took the gun out of his pocket. Ann was behind him, soft-footed. The house was silent. Just three shots, thought Sidney, and

I'm home and dried.

The kitchen door creaked and woke Mike. It also woke Candida who was lying curled up against his back, her thumb in her mouth and the singlet doll clutched to her chest.

As Sid crept in, Mike said contemptuously, 'I thought you'd try that. Put it down, you murdering swine.'

'You were right,' agreed Sidney. 'In a few moments the whole five thou. will be mine.'

'You double-crossing bastard,' spat Ann, standing in the doorway. 'You promised you'd take me, too.'

Mike shifted his concentration from Sidney, to his wife, then lunged at her. But he was too late. Sidney had turned as she spoke and fired at point-blank range into her heart. She fell, and instead of strangling his wife Mike was now cradling her lifeless body in his arms. Sid swung round to take wavering aim at Candida. She shrieked, Mike dropped his wife and dived across the kitchen, shattering the back door with his shoulder. He pushed Candida out into the night. 'Run!' he yelled. 'I'll deal with this bastard.'

Sid fired. The bullet scraped along Mike's arm and buried itself into the mistreated door. Then Mike had hold of the gun hand. Sidney was the smaller and weaker, but he was a tough street fighter. Mike could not get him down.

'Excuse me,' came a clipped voice from the back doorstep. 'Could you possibly hold up the gun hand?'

It was an indescribably dirty young woman. Her face was streaked with blood and mud and her features could not be told, but she had a steady hand and held a pearl-handled revolver with it. Mike gaped briefly, then hauled the gun wrist up until Sid was nearly clear of the ground.

'Thanks,' said Phryne coolly, and placed a neat hole in Sid's wrist. He dropped the gun. Mike knelt on him and tied him up with the length of rope that the surprising young woman produced.

'I really should tie you up, too,' she commented. 'Except that I saw you rescue Candida. We'd better go and find her.'

'I told her to run,' frowned Mike, kicking Sidney in the ribs as an aid to meditation. 'She might not have stopped yet.'

'I've got a lure that will bring her back,' smiled Phryne, and produced the teddybear from the sling.

'Is that Bear?' asked Mike. 'That's good.'

He was contemplating his wife's body.

'I gather she gave you a hard time,' said Phryne.

'It was my own fault,' said Mike ruefully. 'Candida!' he called. 'The lady has brought Bear.'

A small voice spoke from somewhere close. 'I don't believe you. Put him on the step.'

Phryne placed Bear reverently on the step and a rustling was heard in the bushes. A small dirty hand shot out, seized Bear by the leg and dragged him off the step. There was silence. Phryne began to be rather worried.

'Candida? Daddy and Mummy are on their way. They will be here soon. Come inside and er, no, don't come inside. Go out to the car and I'll meet you there.' Phryne heard a faint, relieved sobbing, muffled in teddybear fur.

'Oh, Bear, I knew you'd come. And now Daddy is coming and Mummy is coming and my lollies are coming and the nasty man is caught and the nasty lady is dead.'

Phryne went back into the kitchen. Candida was fine where she was.

'Who are you?' she asked the big man.

'Mike. Mike Herbert. I didn't want to be in this, but I had to support my wife.'

'Did you? Why?'

'She liked pretty things and I couldn't afford to buy them – I lost my job, the factory closed down. I'm a carpenter. She borrowed some money off ... a certain person ... and then she couldn't pay it back, and I couldn't either, so ... the certain person was going to send the boys around, and...'

'Break both her legs, eh? Let's have a look at her. Where did she fall?'

'In the bathroom. I think that she's dead. Poor Ann. She should have been born rich.'

Phryne bent over the body, supine on the oilcloth. She felt for a heartbeat in the cooling breast, and found none. The flesh was clammy and limp against her palm. She stood up and wiped her hands on her trousers.

'I'm sorry,' she said to Mike. 'She can't have felt anything, you know, the bullet drilled her heart.'

Mike knelt, drew his wife's skirt down until it covered her knees, and kissed her gently on the cheek.

'Goodbye, Annie,' Phryne heard him say as she tactfully withdrew. 'I would have done anything to make you happy, but it never worked. You shouldn't have got involved with me. I can't even bury you properly.'

After about ten minutes, Mike came back to the kitchen, where Phryne was bandaging Sid's wrist lest he bleed to an untimely death. He whimpered as he handled him and she observed with pleasure that her aim had been perfect. The hole was in the exact middle of the wrist and had not even chipped a bone. The tendons were, as she had purposed, cut neatly though. He would not use that hand to molest any more children.

Mike came into the kitchen and took Phryne by the shoulder, turning her carefully toward him.

'I never meant to hurt the little girl,' he pleaded.

'Well, she doesn't need you any longer,' commented Phryne. 'So now we must decide what to do. I think that I shall cast you as heroic rescuer. I think I'd better bind up your arm and give you some money. Then you can have a wash and a shave, go home to dear Mrs O'Brien, and report your car stolen. You thought your wife had it, but she's not come back, and you're afraid that something has happened to her. Did you write the note?'

'No,' said Mike through lips numb with astonishment.

'Good. Now let's wash this wound. It's little more than a scratch, just keep it dry.

225

I'll take off this disgusting hat and find my face.'

Phryne put her head under the cold-water tap and scrubbed vigorously. She emerged as a young woman of some distinction with a bleeding cut over one eye. Phryne dabbed at it with her handkerchief.

'You need a bit of sticky plaster,' offered Mike. He found some in the cupboard and applied it neatly. Phryne washed her face again. She was aching all over.

'Henry,' I'll try to give you as much altitude as I can, but I think this is a silly idea,' yelled Bunji as she hauled the plane into another turn. 'You can't even see the ground. The moon's down.'

'I can see that dirty great cross that Phryne's drawn on that road and I'm going to come down right in the middle of it,' said Henry confidently. 'There's no wind. If I haul in the slacks I should drop right on their heads.'

'Oh, all right, old chum, far be it from me to stop a friend anxious to break his neck. Careful as you go over, don't catch anything on the wing. *Merde!*' yelled Bunji. 'Now!'

She had judged it nicely. The man's body fell out of vision. A pale flower blossomed, cutting off her sight of the luminous cross. Right on target. Bunji drank another mouthful of the luke-warm coffee and looked for a place to set down.

Candida, who occasionally did as she was told, had taken Bear out to the road and was sitting quietly on the running board of the Bentley. She looked at the road. It was glowing.

'They must have awful big snails here, Bear, to leave a trail like that. Big enough to ride on. Perhaps we can catch one and ride home.' She yawned. It had been an exciting evening.

Dropping out of the sky into the centre of the snail tracks came a man clad all in leather. Candida froze. He cursed a bit as he loosened the parachute cords and Candida and Bear edged closer. The voice was familiar. Then the man tore off his flying helmet and she saw his face in the lights that were now streaming from the house.

'Daddy!' shrieked Candida, and flew to him, scaling his body and settling back into his embrace. She held him as tight as a limpet for five minutes as he stroked her hair, then she looked up.

'Where have you been?' she asked severely. 'Why did you let those people steal me?'

CHAPTER TWELVE

I met murder on the way
The Mask of Anarchy, P.B. Shelley

Phryne found a bottle of rum and two glasses, and lit her first gasper in hours. She leaned back on the draining board and smoked luxuriously.

'You'd better hit the road, Mike. Don't forget to report the car stolen.'

Mike, dressed in a clean shirt and combed and shaved, looked like a respectable working man. Phryne peeled off a hundred pounds from her wad of notes.

'This should take care of you for a while. I'll look after Candida. Her family will be arriving soon.'

Mike knocked back the rum and pointed at the bundle, which was Sid, on the floor.

'What about him? He'll sing like a canary.'

'I'll take care of him,' said Phryne quietly. Sidney, hearing her, winced.

'Don't look back,' she advised Mike. 'Keep going. There's the right woman, and children, waiting for you yet. If you need any help with a job, come to me.' She tucked her card into his pocket with the money, and let him out the front door.

They were both arrested by the sight of what appeared to be an angel, fallen from the sky. He stood tall and shapely, draped in his billowing wings. Candida and Bear were in his arms.

'Mike,' squealed Candida. 'Daddy's come.'

Mike walked over to her and took her hand.

'Well, everything's worked out then. I've got to go, Candida. I've come to say good-bye.'

Candida, who always associated goodbyes with kisses, turned her cheek. Mike bent and kissed her. Then he took Henry Maldon's hand and shook it firmly. He turned away and walked into the night.

'Mike!' cried Candida, 'you'll get lost in the dark.' But his step did not falter.

Phryne walked over to Henry. 'I think you'd better get off the highway, dear man, or you'll be run over by the rescuers. Excuse me for a moment.' Phryne went back into the kitchen and propped Sid up against a cabinet.

'I want to talk to you,' said Phryne. 'What

will you take for keeping your mouth shut?'

'Why should I? I'll swing as soon as the cops lay their hands on me.'

'Yes, you will. But I might be able to gratify any last wish.'

Her voice contained a hint of perversion. Sidney licked his lips.

'Can you smuggle me a girl before I go to the gallows?'

'I think so,' said Phryne.

Sid wriggled. 'I mean my sort of girl. A child.'

'Perhaps. How old?'

'Twelve at the most.'

Phryne thought of her friend Kiara, a lesbian who got a great kick from getting money out of men. Especially men like Sid. She dressed in a gym slip and looked almost prepubescent. The child-molesters who constituted most of her clientele fuelled her loathing and it would not be the first time her little-girl's body had been purchased by one who was about to die.

From her extensive knowledge of the Underworld Phryne knew that it was no great matter to smuggle anything into a prison. All that was needed were a few timely words and more than a few coins of the realm. She recalled that the orgy which preceded the death of the Canton murderer Jackson had been described to her in great detail by the prison guard who let the three girls in, disguised as prisoners. He said he had stayed to 'supervise' and fend off any inquiries. What had been his name? Briggs, that was it, a Northern Irishman of flexible morality and an ever-open palm. He volunteered for the duty which the other warders avoided; sitting up with the man to be hanged on the morrow. Stranger things than Kiara had been taken into Pentridge for the comfort of those about to die, though the strangest was probably a bushranger's horse. He had wanted to say farewell to it in person.

'I think I can manage that, yes,' she agreed.

'In the death cell?' bargained Sidney. Phryne wondered how long he had been in love with death. Perhaps the desired culmination of his whole career would be his judicial execution at the hands of stronger men. She poured out some rum and helped him drink it. Sidney, dispossessed of his gun, was a pathetic creature.

Ann was less pathetic because she was so very dead. Phryne stood over the corpse and looked down on her. The expression of surprise had faded. She looked now as if she was asleep. The thirsty spirit had gone, presumably back to its maker. Phryne collected up the few personal belongings that pointed to a second man having been present and stuffed them in her pockets. Then she went to sit on the front step and wait for the car. She was aching and bruised and tired out but pleased with the night's work.

Phryne offered Henry a cigarette and lit her own. Candida and Bear were wrapped up in the parachute. They were awake, but warm. The lights of the big car approached. Tree trunks sprank into visibility.

'Here they are at last,' said Phryne. 'I'd kill for a cup of tea. Look, Henry, it's picanninny daylight. The sun will be up in an hour.'

The car drew up, and disgorged Dot, Molly, Jack Leonard and Bunji. They saw two bedraggled figures sitting on the front step of the small house. They were smoking. Next to them was a bundle of white silk, in which one could see a straggling head of pale hair and a Bear.

'Is it all right, Miss?' asked Dot, breaking the silence. Molly flew to Candida, who embraced her frantically.

'Daddy came down out of the sky and the lady brought Bear so I knew that it was all right,' she informed Molly. Then she wriggled down and laid herself out across

Molly's knees.

'What are you doing, Candida Alice?' asked Molly fondly.

'I want my spanking, and then I want my lollies!' said Candida.

Molly laughed, sobbed, and delivered five moderate slaps. Candida sat up and Dot put her bag of lollies into her hands. The child checked through them carefully. The whole threepence work was there, even if somewhat muddy. Candida filled her mouth with mint leaves and began to cry.

They all piled into the car as the sun was rising and took the road for the town. Phryne laughed aloud at the sight of them, all dusty and streaked, and reflected she must be the most bedraggled of them all.

'What's the best hotel in Queenscliff?' she called to Molly.

Molly could not reply because she had unwisely accepted Candida's offer of a toffee and her teeth were glued together.

Henry said, 'The Queenscliff Hotel is the best, but we can't go there looking like this.'

'Yes we can,' said Phryne flatly. 'You should have seen the state in which we once entered the Windsor. I'm positively overdressed by comparison.'

Dot remembered it well. Phryne looked a lot more respectable in her present attire.

They drew up outside the Queenscliff Hotel and climbed the stone steps wearily. There, Phryne's money, charm, and air of authority obtained three rooms, one with a bath, and breakfast as soon as it should be laid. Phryne saw that her guests were settled in front of a hastily-lit fire in the drawing-room then sent a boy out for a roll of brown paper and some string. She wrapped Sid in the paper, using knots taught to her by a young sailor she had loved briefly during World War One. By the time she had fin-ished, only Sid's head was free. With the help of the hotel porter, she then carried Sid to the police station and deposited him on the counter.

The desk-sergeant looked up, blinked, and dropped his pen.

'What's all this about, Miss?'

Phryne sank wearily into a chair and pointed at the uncomfortable felon.

'Read the label,' she said.

The desk-sergeant called for a constable and walked around into the room. He sur-veyed Sid carefully and read the label aloud.

'"For Detective-inspector Jack Robinson, Russell Street, Melbourne. A present from

Phryne Fisher." Aha, we had a message about you, Miss Fisher. They telephoned from Geelong. Every cooperation, they said. You are a respected person, evidently.'

Phryne smiled faintly.

'His name is Sidney Brayshaw, and you've been looking for him for some time, I believe. You'd better get a doctor fairly soon, because I had a little trouble picking him up and he got damaged. Detective-inspector Robinson is going to be furious if you let him bleed to death.'

The sergeant ripped off the paper and led Sidney away. As Sidney was leaving the room, he broke the silence he had maintained throughout his humiliation and called to Phryne 'You better not forget, lady. Remember – I'm not dead yet.'

'You look like you could do with a doctor, too,' suggested the young constable. 'You seem to have taken a bit of a battering. I'll just give the local man a call, shall I?'

'Yes indeed, if you want Sidney to live to hang. He is undoubtedly the most unpleasant person I have ever met in my whole life. How I would love to squeeze the life out of the little rat. Have you heard of him, Constable...'

'Constable Smith, Miss Fisher. I am

astounded that you have come in with Sidney Brayshaw. Why, there's his portrait on the wall,' commented the young man, pointing out a 'Most Wanted' poster. He took it down.

'He ain't wanted any more,' he said. Phryne laughed. The constable did not think he had ever seen a face so drawn. The black hat and the black collar enclosed a countenance as white as marble.

'Where are you staying, Miss? If you don't mind my saying, you look all in.'

'The Queenscliff Hotel. Can you drive my car there? And make me a present of that poster? It will make a perfect souvenir.' Constable Smith, who had a sense of occasion, rolled up the poster and presented it with a bow. Then he vanished behind the desk, presumably to ask permission to leave and to summon the doctor to Sid.

Phryne was almost asleep on her feet when the constable came back. She gave him the keys, suffered herself to be helped into a seat beside him, and by the time Constable Smith had proudly steered the big red car around the corner she was fast asleep.

Thus Phryne made her most impressive entrance, though she missed it at the time, lolling gracefully with her head on a policeman's shoulder. He stalked up the steps in correct uniform, helmet on and every button gleaming.

He stopped at reception and asked the manager,' Where shall I put her?'

The manager did not flick so much as an eyebrow. 'Ah, yes, that is Miss Fisher. Room Six. Her maid has just gone out to purchase some necessaries. Follow me, Constable.' Phryne was carried up the carpeted stairs and laid gently on the bed. Constable Smith took off Phryne's boots and flung the quilt over her.

'Thank you, Constable, I think that will be all,' observed the manager. 'I shall inform her maid that Miss Fisher has returned. I believe that a Mr Jack Leonard was expressing a wish to speak to you.'

The Queenscliff Hotel had been built in those spacious days when an Empire was an Empire, and the rooms were lavishly appointed. Constable Smith brushed past a bowl of winter leaves and berries which took up three square feet and saw the strangest assortment of people he had ever set eyes on, gathered around the largest fireplace he had ever seen. You could have roasted an ox in it, as he told his mates later. There was the chink of dishes in the back parlour as breakfast was laid.

The room contained numerous soft couches and two easy chairs. On one of the couches sat a man in flying gear, playing 'scissors, paper, stone' with a very grubby child in a stained white nightgown. Next to him sat a well-dressed and well-groomed young woman with fiery hair who kept patting the child, as if she was not sure that she was real. Between the child and the sofa back reclined a battered teddybear with a handkerchief around its neck.

In one easy chair sat a plump young woman in leather gear, who had taken a cup of coffee into both hands as though to absorb the heat. She was staring into the fire. In the other easy chair sat the very dapper young man with a thin moustache, who stood up.

'Hello, old chap. That was Miss Fisher I saw you carrying up the stairs just now, wasn't it?'

'Yes,' agreed the constable.

'Is she all right?'

'She fell asleep and I couldn't wake her so I put her to bed. I don't think there is anything wrong with her.'

'Good. She told me that if she didn't succeed in telling you the story I was to inform you that we'll be down to the station after lunch to tell all. By the way, there's a dead

238

woman in a house up the hill,' he gave the address. 'Sidney killed her. I'm sure that he will explain.'

'Thank you, sir,' said the dumbfounded constable. 'I'll see about it right away, sir.'

He left the hotel to go and find his sergeant. What a young constable needs when given this sort of information is a sergeant. However, he had a strong suspicion as to what the sergeant would say.

He was right. He was immediately sent to see if there was a dead woman in the house. There was.

Dot had found that the lady who kept the drapers shop lived over her premises, and Dot knocked until a sleepy voice replied that she was coming. At last the door opened.

'Well?' asked Mrs Draper.

'I need a lot of things for three ladies who are benighted in the area,' said Dot. Mrs Draper opened the shop door and switched on the light.

'You look for what you want, dear,' she said kindly. 'I'll just go and make me tea.'

She tottered off. Dot selected a light travelling bag and found a nightgown and a pair of soft, black velvet slippers. Phryne's trousers were all very well but one could not dine in them. Dot took a black skirt in a size W for

Bunji and in SSW for Phryne; bought a loose white blouse with dolman sleeves and a bright red jersey top, three gentlemen's shirts and socks and undergarments and three sets of stockings and undies for the ladies. Then she remembered herself and added one more of each. At the back of the shop she spied a quaint, beaded cap, with a long scarf hanging from it. She bought a feather cockade for the black cloche and remembered Bunji's flying boots at the last moment and bought her a pair of slippers, too. She wrestled this mountain of purchases onto the counter and went in search of the draper.

Placidly, the old woman added up the astronomical total, checked it, and gave Dot change. She agreed that the things would be sent instantly to the Queenscliff Hotel and saw her customer to the door, which she locked behind her. Then she chose a comfortable bit of floor and fainted.

Dot hurried back to the hotel. She had the nightgown and slippers in the light bag, and the thought of a cup of tea spurred her on. An aeroplane was attracting a crowd down on the foreshore, and a stern lifeboat man was warning the children away.

Dot ran up the steps and was just in time

for breakfast.

'Oh, I say, pity that Phryne is missing this,' opined Jack Leonard. Dot thought so, too. She went up to Room Six and opened the door. Phryne was half-awake.

'What's that delicious smell, Dot? I've had the most amazing dream. I was clinging on to the back of a car ... hang on. That wasn't a dream. Dot, where are we?'

'Queenscliff Hotel, Miss, and breakfast is waiting. Why not wash your face and brush your hair and come down? I've never seen a breakfast like it.'

The Queenscliff Hotel was famed for its breakfasts. Phryne put on the black slippers and brushed her hair as ordered. She and Dot descended into a cloud of steam savoury enough to make a glutton swoon. Phryne's stomach growled reproachfully. Dot felt almost faint with hunger. They passed the formal dining-room and the cocktail bar and burst into the back parlour at something not too short of a run. Jack Leonard gave a cheer as Phryne came in and supplied her with a big plate.

'Now, Phryne, you must keep up your strength. There won't always be policemen to carry you around.'

'So I didn't dream the policeman either.

How odd.'

'What would you like?' asked Jack, leading her to a long row of silver chafing dishes. 'There are kidneys and devilled ham in this one, scrambled eggs in this one, mushrooms in this one, sausages, rissoles, fried eggs and they can make you an omelette in a moment.'

'This is too much. Get me a bit of everything, Jack, and bless you.'

Phryne sat down at a small table. A waiter took her order for tea and offered her a newspaper, which she waved away. When furnishing the hotel someone had bought a job lot of life-size negro figures made of wood or paper mache. At the feet of the one with the gold turban sat Candida, eating fruit compote with perfect equanimity. Phryne raised an eyebrow at Molly.

'She says that the poor man must be lonely, so she's gone to keep him company,' Molly explained. 'Have some of this compote, it's marvellous. Essence of summer. I wonder where they found melons, pineapple and strawberries at this time of the year?'

Jack placed Phryne's plate before her and she had demolished it, with three slices of toast and two cups of tea before he had time to complete one across in the *Times* cross-word. Phryne went back to the buffet and gave herself more bacon, scrambled eggs, mushrooms and kedgeree. This she ate with two slices of toast, Dot had found the diversity of things to eat miraculous. All that food! She picked at everything.

Phryne tried the fruit and found it delight-ful, then stood up and stretched.

'I bags first bath,' she said, and Dot raced after her as she fled up the stairs.

Ten minutes later she was lying in a hot bath and Dot was soaping her feet. She was so stiff that she could not possibly have reached them.

'Oh, your poor toes, Miss!'

'I suppose it isn't any use asking you to call me Phryne, is it, Dot?'

'No. It ain't right. And you are changing the subject. You've bruised them toes so that you won't be able to put a shoe on your feet for a week. You've cut your hands and there's a little cut on your brow. It won't cause a scar, Miss,' commented Dot. 'Let me have your foot again. I've sent your clothes to be cleaned, and they say they'll be back this afternoon. Miss Candida's as well. Mrs Maldon wants to get rid of that nightgown. I didn't think of buying a new one for her.

243

That's better, Miss. Hang on to my hand and ... up we go!'

Dot dried Phryne, clad her in the night-gown, and put her to bed between clean sheets.

Dot took a bath, replaced her chemise, and lay down in her own bed for some sleep. She was rather worn out from worrying about Phryne and Candida and Henry and Bunji.

The Maldons had been given a room with a bath, and the hotel had provided a cot draped with white muslin. Candida was impressed with it. It resembled the cradle of the Princess's baby in the *Blue Fairy Book*. She was a cleanly little girl and was delighted to see how much dirt coloured the water. When she was finally ready and wrapped up in several towels, her father claimed the bath and firmly shut the door.

Candida surveyed the room. It was lovely. She admired the gold chandelier, and the swags of ivy picked out in gold leaf on the high ceilings. The French windows opened onto the balcony and through them she could see the sea. The heavy curtains of oyster-grey silk had been elaborately draped in order to frame the view. In front of the window was a carved blackwood loveseat, a round low table with a bowl of roses and three delicate-legged chairs. There was an escritoire and matching chair on one side of the fire and a washstand on the other.

The great bed was of brass and stood at least two feet off the floor. It was heaped with pillows. Candida climbed up and bounced experimentally.

Molly darkened the windows and took off most of her clothes. She got into the bed and found that Bear and Candida were already there.

'Bear wants to know when we are going home.'

'Tomorrow morning. We are just going to have a little sleep. Daddy will be here in a moment. Do you want to sleep in the cot?'

'Me?' asked Candida indignantly. 'It's for a baby.'

Molly smiled and closed her eyes. When Henry came out of the bathroom, he found both of his women fast asleep.

Phryne woke refreshed and stiff at two o'clock. Dot was still sleeping. The blind let through a little cool winter light, and she could hear the sea. She inspected the clothes that Dot had bought, especially the odd little hat. She put it on and peeped into the mirror. It was striking. The beads added weight, so that it sat down well upon her head. She looped the scarf around her throat.

'O woman of mystery,' she said blowing a kiss to her reflection. She put on the black skirt and the red jersey top, then went downstairs to see if any of the rest of her party were awake.

The desk clerk smiled at her.

'The rest of them have gone for a walk on the shore, Miss Fisher,' he said respectfully. 'The little girl insisted.'

Phryne smiled. Candida was prone to insist. She gathered up her skirt and went down the steps and across the road, following the path to the pier.

It was a cold day, and few people were on the foreshore. Phryne found Candida, her parents, Bunji and Jack sitting on the sand and making rather ineffectual castles.

'That's not right,' said Candida as her castle dissolved before a strong lee wind. 'Make me an aeroplane, Uncle Jack.'

Jack Leonard moved down the beach a little and found that the damper sand held its shape better. Bunji came with him to advise.

'Make a Fokker,' she suggested. 'Did you see her, Phryne? I had to put her down on the sand. Had a bit of a struggle persuading the old girl to stop, seemed to want to go on into the waves, and that wouldn't have done, you know. The lifeguard was delighted to watch it for me. He was in the Royal Flying Corps. Fascinating old bird. I think the nose ought to be a bit longer, Jack.'

Jack obediently lengthened the nose. Candida found suitable pebbles for the finer details. Molly and Henry were sitting on a cold stone step. Molly was leaning back into Henry's embrace. He had his head on her shoulder. Phryne was about to withdraw when Molly held out a hand.

'We owe it all to you, Phryne. We don't know how to repay you.'

'There's no need to repay me. I wouldn't have missed it for worlds. The really brave person in this was Bunji. Henry must have told you what a good flyer she is.'

'Great skill,' agreed Henry. 'She can scent the air currents, I reckon. Who is this Mike that Candida keeps talking about?'

'Did you read the Sherlock Holmes stories?' asked Phryne, seating herself at Henry's feet.

'Yes, of course.'

'"I think we must have an amnesty in that direction"' quoted Phryne. 'He was dragged into the plot by his revolting wife. The monster I delivered to the cops this morning was the prime mover. When Sidney shot the wife and was trying to shoot Candida, Mike realized that he couldn't go along with it, shoved Candida out into the garden and told her to run. Then he attacked Sid. That's where I came in. I shot Sid in the wrist and had a conference with Mike. He saved Candida's life. Even if we all gave character evidence for him he'd be looking at ten years in the pen. So I gave him a hundred quid and told him to go home and report his car stolen. They will suspect him, but they won't be able to prove anything. He is a good chap, Henry met him.'

'So it was Mike who kissed Candida good-bye? I'm glad that I met him. I owe him a great deal.'

'I told him to get in touch with me if he couldn't get a job. If he does, I'll turn him over to you.'

'You did well, Phryne. It would have been awful to have to give evidence against him.'

Molly's eyes strayed to Candida, engaged in making wheels for the plane. The child was dressed in her blue frock, and had Bear secured to her back with a handkerchief.

'I don't think she's suffered too much,' said Phryne, 'though she'll probably have nightmares. She didn't see the woman fall

248

when she was shot and she escaped Siddy's attentions.'

'I was wondering about that. He's a child-molester, isn't he?' asked Henry. 'I ... didn't know how to ask her.'

'No need. He may have had designs on her originally, but when she came out from under the ether Sid told me that she was sick all over him.'

Henry laughed aloud. 'That's my girl!'

Dinner in the formal dining-room was hilarious. Phryne purchased good champagne and after a while everyone was happy. The food was excellent, from the entree of cream of pumpkin soup, through an exquisite cheese souffle, a *filet mignon à chasseur,* and sherberts made of peach, nectarine, pomegranate, lemon, orange and grapefruit. The coffee was fragrant and the handmade chocolates remarkable.

Phryne, who had bagged the quaint hat, ate as though she had been fasting for some months. Dot was freshly surprised at each course. Candida, who had been allowed to stay up by special permission, had presided over the ceremonial burning of the night-gown, the last trace of her captivity. She was engaged in assisting Bear to eat his chocolates. Golden candlelight from the tall sconces glittered off the massive silver epergnes and dishes; the log fire burned brightly. Tall vases of lilies and gum tips lent the air a delicate scent. Of all endings to adventure, this was the best possible.

'To Candida!' cried Phryne, and raised her glass. Uncle Jack allowed the child to take a sip from his glass. The bubbles tickled her nose. She chuckled. She knew that it was the custom to respond to a toast. She clutched Bear close to give him confidence, and stood up on her chair.

'Uncle Jack, Aunty Bunji, Mummy, Daddy, Dot and Phryne,', she began. The table was silent. Candida was overcome with sudden affection.

'Thank you for finding me and bringing me Bear,' she said, then launched herself into Phryne's arms, and kissed her moistly on the cheek.

CHAPTER THIRTEEN

He that dies pays all debts
The Tempest, Shakespeare

Returned in good order to Melbourne, Phryne spent Thursday afternoon cleaning the car with Mr Butler's assistance. She gave her household an edited account of her adventures, and did not go out until Thursday afternoon to St Kilda. She wanted to find Klara. As Klara was locally notorious, this did not prove difficult.

A thin little gutter sparrow sat in a café, staring into an empty cup of tea. She looked up as Phryne walked in and smiled with genuine tenderness.

'Phryne! Come and buy me some tea. I'm parched. Got a job for me?'

Phryne bought the tea, which she would not have touched for quids, and explained. Ancient eyes started out of a childish face.

'And they'll kill him the next day?'

'Yes.'

'I'll do it for ten quid. If I didn't have to

make a living I'd do it for nothing. Sidney Brayshaw, eh? Bonzer. Will you make the arrangements?'

'Can you? I don't know if Briggs is still at Pentridge.'

'Sure. Give me another twenty to square them.'

Phryne produced the money.

'You won't fail me, Klara? I gave my word.'

'No. I'll not fail,' promised Klara, tracing a cross with a grubby forefinger on the flat breast of her gym tunic. Phryne left quickly. She found Klara unsettling.

Thursday night was appointed for Phryne's seduction of the delightful Dr Fielding. It was not until Mrs Butler was asking her what she fancied for dinner that she remembered.

'Oh, hell, I forgot. Mrs B., I asked that nice young doctor to dinner.'

'You have been busy lately, Miss,' agreed Mrs Butler. 'So we won't quarrel about it this time.'

Phryne took the hint and smiled. 'I hope that there won't be a next time,' she said pleasantly. 'Can you manage a simple, light dinner?'

'Vegetable soup, lamb chops, green beans,

pommes de terre Anna? Apple pie and cream?' suggested Mrs Butler.

'Good. Very nice. Then coffee and liqueurs in my sitting-room upstairs. Can Mr B. take care of the fire? And leave the woodbox full. After he's brought the coffee, Mrs B. I don't want to be disturbed.'

Mrs Butler pursed her lips and nodded. Phryne wondered if the two of them were going to give notice in the morning. Assuming, of course, that the doctor was amenable to seduction.

Phryne bathed luxuriously and dressed carefully in a loose, warm velvet from *Erté*. It was black, with deep lapin cuffs and collar and a six-inch band of fur around the hem. She brushed her hair vigorously and applied just a little rouge.

Dot assisted her into the gown and knelt to adjust the soft Russian boots around Phryne's slim ankles.

'You fancy your chances, Miss?'

'Yes, I do. He's clumsy, but rather endearing, don't you think?'

'You be careful,' warned Dot. 'This one's an Aussie. They got different ideas about their girls, not like them Russians.'

'And Italians,' agreed Phryne. 'I'll be careful, Dot. Are you going out or staying in?'

'I'm staying in,' said Dot, giving the boot-lace a final tug. 'I've been to the library and I'm going to read and listen to the wireless. I won't disturb you, Miss. I can come and go by my own stair.'

'I hope that this doesn't upset you,' said Phryne. 'Or the Butlers.'

'They'll be sweet,' said Dot. 'Just like I was. It's a bit of a shock at first, but you get used to it. Have a nice time, Miss,' and Dot, innocent of any envy, went down to take her own dinner with the Butlers. Phryne smoked one gasper after another, worrying. Dot was right. Australian men were different. She did not want to get involved in an emotional relationship. She had no patience with dependence and no understanding of jealousy.

She heard the doorbell ring, and sailed downstairs to meet her guest, with outward poise and inward qualms.

He really was beautiful, she reflected as he escorted her into the dining-room. He had pale skin, curly brown hair, was well-built and tall. Phryne took her seat and accepted a glass of white wine from Mr Butler. The young man contrived by a miracle not to knock over the vase of ferns in the centre of the table and smiled ruefully.

'I'm afraid I'm still clumsy, Miss Fisher.'

'Really, you must call me Phryne. I'm not your patient, Dr Fielding.'

'Then you must call me Mark.'

'You haven't been a doctor long, I gather. Why did you choose medicine?'

This was always a safe question to ask any professional. Soup was served. It was good – perhaps a little too much celery. Mark Fielding ate fast, as though he was about to be called away at any moment.

'I want to be useful,' said Mark Fielding. 'I want to heal the hurts of the world.' He laid down his spoon. 'That sounds silly, doesn't it? But there is such a lot of pain and suffering, and I want to ease it. I work with old Dr Dorset, he has great experience, but he's a cynical old man. He says that everyone in the world has ulterior motives. What do you think?'

Phryne took in a sharp breath as the unreadable brown eyes flicked sidelong to look at her. Yes, she could believe it. Her own motives were nothing to boast of.

The excellent dinner concluded, Phryne lured Mark upstairs with a promise of coffee and kirsch. She accepted the tray from Mr Butler, observed that the woodbox next to the fire had been replenished, and gave him a conspiratorial smile.

'I shan't want you again tonight, Mr B.,' she said. 'Sleep well.'

'You too, Miss Fisher,' he replied with perfect gravity, and chuckled all the way down the stairs.

'I know what she is, Mrs B.,' he said at the kitchen door. 'She's a vamp.'

'Ah, well,' sighed his wife. 'At least it ain't like the last place. Young men are clean about the house. It's better than the old gentleman's greyhounds.'

Thereafter Phryne's household always referred to her lovers as 'the pets'.

Mark Fielding leaned back into the feathery embrace of a low, comfortable sofa in front of a bright fire.

'Oh, this is nice,' he sighed. 'Listen to that wind outside. It's beginning to rain, too. I wish I didn't have to go home ... I mean,' he corrected himself hurriedly, 'I mean...'

'You don't have to go home,' said Phryne calmly. 'I wouldn't turn a dog out on a night like this. Stay with me, Mark. It's warm in here.'

She was lying at full length on the hearth rug, prone, with her chin cupped in her hands, the short cap of black hair swung forward to hide her face. She had not looked away from the fire as she spoke. The young doctor was astonished. He had never been propositioned by a woman before.

He glanced around the room. Every surface was velvety, textured, soft. The pinkish mirror wreathed in vine leaves reflected his face crowned with a garland. He tried to sit up but the sofa was unwilling to release him. He sipped the remains of his kirsch and yielded up his body to fate.

'It's kismet,' he said softly, as Phryne gathered her gown about her and pulled him down into her arms.

Phryne closed her eyes as the red mouth came down onto hers, the lips parted, then the mouth moved down her throat to the open collar of the velvet gown. For such a clumsy young man, Mark Fielding removed a lady's clothes with startling skill.

Phryne, naked, and stretched out in a pool of velvet and fur, drowsed up out of a fiery trance to glimpse the flash of thigh and buttock and he slid down to lie beside her.

She reached up to catch her fingers in the curly hair, as silky as embroidery floss, and bring the face down for her kiss. As he slid his strong hands between fur and skin to gather her close, he whispered. 'Phryne, are you sure?'

Phryne had seized him, locking his waist

with her thighs. She was sure.

Mark abandoned himself to unimagined delights. The heat of the fire caressed his skin. The scent of Phryne's breasts and her hair, musky and amorous, almost drowned him in sweetness.

When Phryne awoke, the fire was out, and someone seemed to have amputated her legs at the hips. She groaned and tried to sit up. The numbness was explained by the weight of the beautiful young man asleep on top of her. Phryne shook him, laughing and shivering. 'Mark, wake up, you're crushing me.'

Mark Fielding was dragged up out of a deep dream by the hand on his shoulder.

'It must be Mrs Murphy's baby,' he murmured. 'All right, I'll be down in a mm ... no wait, what ... oh, Phryne,' he remembered suddenly, shifted his weight, and hauled her into his arms. 'Oh, my dear girl, how cold you are, and how cold I am, too.'

'We fell asleep, and I think we ought to go to bed before we catch our death. You'll have to carry me,' said Phryne smugly. 'I'm numb.'

Mark staggered up, stamped a few times to recover the use of his feet, then lifted Phryne without effort and bore her into the bedroom. He flung her into the huge bed then dived in after her. The invaluable Mrs B. had left a hot waterbottle and they snuggled close together, limbs entwined, and began to thaw into life. Oddly enough, when Mark Fielding was to think of the amazing Phryne Fisher, that was the moment he remembered as being the most intensely erotic.

The morning of Miss McNaughton's party dawned, cold and bright. Phryne did not see it. She breakfasted in bed with Dr Fielding, sharing toast and buttery kisses. He left at nine, begging to be allowed to return that night.

Phryne had obtained Detective-inspector Benton's solemn promise that he would attend Miss McNaughton's party and Jillian Henderson had rather warily agreed to come. Bert and Cec reported that they had completed their investigations and there was only Miss Wilson left to interview.

Phryne decided to ring her. She found the number and a light, feminine voice identified herself as Margaret Wilson.

'Miss Wilson, this relates to the complaint you made to the police last week.'

'That horrid old man stole my clothes when I was swimming!' exclaimed Miss Wilson. 'I was so mad that I went straight to the police, even though I only had my bathing costume on. But that is all fixed. They lent me a coat to go home in, and the next day I got my clothes back.'

'Think carefully. Did you pass anyone on that path?'

'Yes, Bill McNaughton. I was going to ask him to help me but he was in one of his rages, and there is not a lot of percentage to be got out of Bill when he's like that.'

'Miss Wilson, where have you been all week?'

'In retreat, at Daylesford. I go every year. Why?'

'Bill's father was murdered. You are the only person who can say that Bill was on that path.'

'Lord! Poor Bill. I must go and make a statement, then. Should I go now?'

'No. The slops had their chance. Can you come to Miss McNaughton's children's party tomorrow?'

'Yes, of course. Will that help?'

'About twelve. Do you know Miss Mc-Naughton?'

'Oh, yes, we went to school together. Why didn't Bill say that he saw me?'

'He didn't remember your name.'

'Isn't that just like Bill. He never even

looked at his sister's friends. All right, Miss Fisher, I shall be there tomorrow. Thank you,' said Miss Wilson, and hung up.

Phryne and Dot drove along the gravelled drive and left the car in the carriage yard. The front door was open and there was the sound of someone playing the piano with more exuberance than skill. The sound of running feet echoed down the hall.

Mabel showed Phryne in and took her coat. The house was clean and decorated with balloons and streamers.

'We've put the table in the conservatory, Miss Fisher. It's out the back. The room with the stone floor. That policeman has arrived. So has Miss Wilson from around the corner, two of your agents, and a lady lawyer called Miss Henderson.'

'How are things now, Mabel?'

'Ever so much better, Miss,' said Mabel, lowering her voice. 'Mr Bill hasn't had a single rage, and Mr Paolo is charming. Such a nice man, for a foreigner. He's playing the piano at the moment so the children can play musical chairs. Come out, Miss, it's such a pretty sight.'

It was. The conservatory was a big block added on to the back of the house. It was floored with black slate and masses of plants were suspended from the beams. Paolo was thumping wildly on a baby grand piano looking like a fatherly faun. A scatter of children were running around a diminishing number of chairs. Presiding over the ginger-beer, orange-pop, lemonade and a quiet tray of cocktails was Mrs McNaughton. Phryne hardly knew her. Her cheeks were flushed and she was wearing a paper hat. With her was a tall man in a Harris tweed coat. He had a moustache of impressive proportions and held a whisky and soda in his left hand. His right hand was missing and the tweed sleeve was neatly pinned up. This was Gerald. He smiled dotingly at Mrs McNaughton and raised his glass to Phryne.

Jillian Henderson was deep in converse with Amelia over the properties of begonias and tuberoses, for which she had a passion. Detective-inspector Benton sat on the edge of the chair looking exquisitely uncomfortable. The children gave him uneasy glances. They knew a cop when they saw one.

Bert and Cec, having been provided with beer, were seated at a cast-iron table, watching the game with approval.

After a final burst of Chopin, Jim was left in regal possession of the last chair. He accepted the prize penny, and gave it to Elsie to store in her drawers.

Phryne stepped into the middle of the floor and clapped her hands.

'Before we have lunch, we are going to play a new game,' she told the children and watching adults. 'The game is called, "Murder".'

There was a buzz of excitement. Bill came in from the garden, saw Margaret Wilson, and roared, 'Margaret Wilson! I knew I'd seen that red bathing costume before.'

'Bill, join in the procession,' ordered Phryne. 'Bert and Cec, you bring the kids. It will be all right. I promise. Come along.'

'Where are we going?' asked Dot.

'To the tennis-court,' said Phryne. She led her congregation across the manicured grass until they all stood under the tree.

'When I spoke to you on this spot last week, Benton, I asked you two good questions, and you didn't listen to them. Do you remember what they were?'

'Where did the rock come from, and why was the deceased on the tennis-court in his street shoes. Yes, I remember. I said that the fact that the stone was imported showed that the crime was premeditated, and that the place was chosen to be out of sight of the road.'

'Yes. You were bending the facts to fit your theory. This is almost always fatal. Now I did not have a theory so I approached the matter with an open mind. Where did the rock come from? Bert?'

'It's the same as the ones in Paris St, Miss. They are taking up the old kerb-stones and replacing them with cement. They've been there a while, and there's clover growing over them.'

'Good. What did you find on the murder weapon, Benton?'

'A clover burr, hemp, chewy, and some grass,' said Benton.

'Good. Now it struck me that whoever imported the stone might have been playing a game. What game have all the children been playing since Luxor was found?'

She pointed at Jim. He faltered. 'Pyramids, Miss.'

'Cec will now take us to where he found the rope.'

Cec led the way, and revealed the pile of bluestone pitchers. They had been tumbled over the fence, and under them was revealed the cache of Pharoah's treasures, food for the afterlife in the form of a licorice block and pictures of his royal relatives, transport and even slaves with white kilts. Amelia stared at them, paling to the whiteness of chalk. Paolo took her arm, worried.

'What were these children doing when you saw them yesterday, Bert?'

'Trying to wrap up an old girl's cat as a mummy,' chuckled Bert. 'They had all the bandages but the cat wouldn't play.'

'Jim, tell us what you were playing here when Mr McNaughton caught you.'

'Pyramids,' whispered Jim. 'We took the tyre down and Mickey was up the tree. We was hauling the stones up like the pictures said. It worked bonzer, too. We had four stones for each side of the square, and we almost finished it when...'

'Exactly. Why was the deceased wearing street shoes? He saw from his drive a gaggle of street children desecrating his sacred turf. And after he had strictly forbidden his daughter to allow them on the property. What did he do? He strode across here and bellowed in his most terrifying voice that they should clear off. Mickey was up in the tree, holding the rope to which the top stone was attached. The deceased halted directly under him and Mickey was so terrified that he let the stone go. Then he fell off the tree and ran for his life. Is that right?'

Jim nodded. Mickey began to howl. Bert, who had been expecting this, thrust a huge toffee apple into the gaping maw.

'The kids all ran away as fast as they could go. Eh, Jimmy?'

Jimmy grinned, remembering that flight over the fence and down the valley, into the safety of their favourite box-thorn.

'So, you see, the blow was delivered by a more powerful force than man. It was gravity that murdered McNaughton. That pitcher weighs about twenty pounds and it fell some three feet. Enough to cave in any skull. So McNaughton dies as he had lived; a mean old cuss.'

'How did the tyre get back, then?'

'Ah. In the house, Miss Amelia is told that her brother has been pacing about uttering threats against her father before stamping off down the valley. She goes to look for him. There is her father, lying in the grass, perfectly dead. She does not understand the significance of the stones. She leaps to the conclusion that her brother has killed her father. She takes the bluestones and dumps them over the wall, with the tomb treasures. She unties the rope and throws it away. She is wearing soft house shoes so she leaves no footmark. Then she takes a new piece of rope and re-hangs the tyre. The children's pulley has fallen naturally into the groove carved in the bark by the swing, so there is no other sign of their presence. She intends to discover the body the next day, but Daniel the spaniel is not going to be denied. Danny knows a dead body when he sees one. So the death is revealed sooner than she expected. Is that what happened, Amelia?'

Paolo gave her an affectionate shake.

'Why did you not tell me foolish one? I would have helped you. You must not carry stones – you will spoil your fingers.'

Bill, congested with emotion, said, 'Amelia! Is this true?'

'Yes, Bill.'

'Sporting of you, old girl,' he mumbled. Amelia smiled. Mrs McNaughton, who was a little slow, finally reached her conclusion.

'Then it was an accident.'

'Yes, Mother.'

'Bill didn't kill him.'

'No, Mother.'

'In fact, no one killed him!'

'That is right, Mrs McNaughton,' agreed Detective-inspector Benton. 'Much as I hate to admit it.'

'Good. I also have a witness to Bill's walk. It can be confirmed by consulting the daybook in Kew police station. You should have checked. This is she – Miss Wilson.'

Margaret Wilson was a sturdy, tanned, straightforward young woman, who had clearly never lied in her life.

'I passed Bill on that path at four,' she stated. 'He has met me before, but I must have made no impression on him, which is a pity.'

Bill protested incoherently. 'No, Margaret, don't think that. I had a lot on my mind. I was in a mood. Don't think that I...' He trailed off and blushed.

Miss Wilson took his arm.

'Well. Is this the end of the game?' asked Paolo.

'Ask the detective-inspector,' said Phryne.

'Is it?' Paolo hugged his fiancé close. 'Are you going to arrest the girl for loyalty to her brother? Surely that would not be a good deed. And he died by his own act. Had he not ambushed these children he would be alive today, which would not be a good idea.'

'No charges will be laid against Miss Mc-Naughton or the kids,' said the detective-inspector glumly.

'Then I would like to announce that Miss McNaughton has agreed to be my wife and I trust that we shall see you all at the wedding, including you, *scugnizzi*. If you wash your faces first. Since my wife will not have any money from the estate of her father no aspersions can be cast at us.'

'That's what you think,' commented Jillian. 'That clause is invalid. Void for being contrary to public policy. She will get the money without the condition, as will Mrs McNaughton. I know the solicitor who drew up that will. Poor thing. He told the old man all about what would happen if it was challenged, but all he would say was, "They'd never dare". Unpleasant person. So if I feel like casting the odd aspersion at you, Paolo, I shall cast them.'

'Under the circumstances you are welcome, *Signorina Avvocata*. Shall we also invite this so-tedious policeman to our wedding, *cara?*'

'Yes,' said Amelia. 'I want to paint him.'

They all went to lunch, well and truly satisfied.

'Have another cocktail,' suggested Phryne to the detective-inspector. 'Theories are like that. At least I didn't expose you through my old friend who works for "The Hawklet", did I?

The policeman paled, and gulped the cocktail.

The street children were seated at the buffet, with all their favourite foods within reach. Lucy had uncorked Mickey from his apple and was feeding him cream cake while she ate a fat chocolate bar in neat, mouselike nibbles. Jim and Elsie were up to their eyes in rainbow jelly. Janey was applying raspberry vinegar to her face and the front of her frock. The violent death of McNaughton did not seem to be haunting them.

Bert lifted his beer in a toast to Cec, who could not move because Amelia was sketching him and asking if he had a Scandinavian grandparent. Phryne had snared a lamington out of sheer nostalgia and was wondering if Margaret Wilson really wanted Bill McNaughton, in view of his lousy heredity.

Someone seized her arm in an iron grip.

'Damn you, Phryne,' hissed Jillian Henderson. 'You've gone and lost me my murder!'

The publishers hope that this book has given you enjoyable reading. Large Print Books are especially designed to be as easy to see and hold as possible. If you wish a complete list of our books please ask at your local library or write directly to:

Magna Large Print Books
Magna House, Long Preston,
Skipton, North Yorkshire.
BD23 4ND

This Large Print Book, for people
who cannot read normal print,
is published under the auspices of

THE ULVERSCROFT FOUNDATION

APL		CCS	
Cen		Ear	
Mob		Cou	
ALL		Jub	
WH		CHE	
Ald		Bel	
Fin		Fol	
Can		STO	
Til		HCL	